A war that needed
to be finished

Once again Mother Blessing knew the fury of being thwarted by people for whom she had no respect. Those meddling teenagers should have fallen immediately before the might of her creation. Instead, her simulacrum had been defeated by that boy. . . .

So she was angry with them, these children who had defeated her far too often, considering who and what they were. Insignificant insects who muddled along by accident and who needed to be stamped out. They would pay the price, though—once Season was no longer a problem, these others would taste her revenge too, and they would find it painful indeed. . . .

Mother Blessing would not trust a simulacrum to do the whole job this time. So close to Season, she had to be on the scene in person, just in case.

She would leave immediately. This was a war that needed to be finished, and with the Convocation almost upon them, the end had to come soon.

As the seasons change, so does Kerry. . . .
Check out the other installments
in the Witch Season series:

Summer

Fall

Winter

witch
season

SPRING

JEFF MARIOTTE

Simon Pulse
New York London Toronto Sydney

This one's for Michelle, for seeing it through.
Thanks, Michelle!

This book is a work of fiction. Any references to historical events, real people, or real locales are used fictitiously. Other names, characters, places, and incidents are the product of the author's imagination, and any resemblance to actual events or locales or persons, living or dead, is entirely coincidental.

ᴟSIMON PULSE
An imprint of Simon & Schuster
Children's Publishing Division
1230 Avenue of the Americas, New York, NY 10020

Copyright © 2005 by Jeff Mariotte
All rights reserved, including the right of
reproduction in whole or in part in any form.

SIMON PULSE and colophon are registered
trademarks of Simon & Schuster, Inc.

Designed by Ann Zeak
The text of this book was set in Bembo.

Manufactured in the United States of America
First Simon Pulse edition April 2005
10 9 8 7 6 5 4 3 2 1

Library of Congress Control Number 2004116260

ISBN 0-689-86726-3

A lot of changes have come and gone during the process of writing these books. I need to thank those who helped make it all happen and allowed me to keep working on them, including Maryelizabeth, Holly, Dave, Cindy, Larry, Anne, Vince, Christine, Patrick, Chris, and of course all the great people at Simon Pulse, and booksellers everywhere who took a chance on them. Thanks to all of you.

SPRING

Kerry Profitt's diary, December 26.

It's hard to describe exactly what I was feeling, standing there beside the road that led down to Berlin, New Hampshire, looking at the expressions on the faces of my friends and realizing that they were afraid of me.

Because we're talking about *me*. Not only am I the kind of person who wouldn't, as they say, hurt a fly, I'm the kind who the fly could probably beat up. Old stringbean Profitt, that's me. Arms more like Minnie Mouse than Popeye.

Lately, however, I've learned that one doesn't have to be all buff and weight—liftery to be powerful. And it's that kind of power—the kind that comes from understanding one's relationship to the ebb and flow of natural forces—that made Brandy, Rebecca, and Scott so afraid of me. They saw me with Season Howe—whom they had known only as a hated enemy—battling Mother Blessing's simulacra.

And since one of those simulacra had come up from Berlin in the car with my buds, while I was coming down the selfsame mountainside in a car with Season, they unsurprisingly assumed that I had gone over to Season's side.

Which, to be fair, I had.

But also to be fair, Season isn't the monster they thought she was. And Mother Blessing, whom they still believed was trustworthy, is a monster.

All in all, a confusing situation. Which didn't make it any easier to look at their faces and know they feared me.

I did what I had to do at that minute. Mentally and physically drained as I was from the fight, I made like a cross between an auctioneer and Dr. Phil and fast-talked them out of panicking and running away. Then I persuaded them to follow us, in Scott's car, back up the hill to Season's cabin. Once we got there, Season made us some hot spiced apple cider while I laid the whole story out for them—starting at the beginning, which was 1704 and the destruction of Slocumb, Virginia. I told them how Daniel Blessing had always been told by his mother that it was Season who destroyed Slocumb, and how when Daniel and his twin brother Abraham were old enough, Mother Blessing sent them out on their quest for revenge. Or *her* quest, to be more precise. But it turns out that Mother Blessing is a stinking liar, and she's spent all these years blaming Season for something she did herself. In the process, she cost both of her sons their lives, and got our friends Mace and Josh killed too.

Okay, technically, Season is the one who killed Mace. She doesn't get off the hook for that one so easily. But the winds of war, I think somebody once said, can shift in an instant. When she killed Mace, he had been hooked up with us and we were hooked up with Daniel and Daniel was trying to kill Season. So self-defense? Kind of hard to argue with.

In the end, I must have been persuasive. Scott and Rebecca were easy, of course—Scott because he majorly crushes on me, and Rebecca because she always wants to believe the best of anybody. Brandy was tougher, as I had known she would be. But finally she came over to my side as well. Season helped—she speaks well for herself, articulate and bright and convincing. By the end of it they had all agreed to spend the night there, in the cabin, with the under-standing that we'd move out by first light. It isn't safe here anymore, Season told us. Mother Blessing had been able to track us this far, had even been able to get one of her magically constructed pseudo-men to join up with them. She was getting too close, and we had to abandon this hidey-hole and go somewhere else.

The hugs and kisses and tears that should have accompanied our reunion—the first time we had all been together since Josh's death in Las Vegas—came then, at the end of the evening instead of the begin-ning. We were all wrung out emotionally by then, all exhausted. With the prospect of a very early morning facing us, we went to our assigned sleeping areas—I'm still in the bed I've been in since Christmas Eve—to get some shut-eye.

Except of course, me being me, a day like this requires some journaling time as well. But sunup is going to feel awfully early, so I should probably fold up the trusty laptop and actually shut that afore-mentioned eye.

Both of them, even.

More later.

K.

1

In the morning Season pounded on the door to her room, and Kerry started, as surprised as if someone had lit a firecracker under her feet. She sat up in bed, took stock quickly of where she was, rubbed her bleary eyes. Another four hours of unconsciousness would have been good, another six even better. Christmas day had been relaxing, but it was bookended by days that were anything but, and she was feeling the strain.

She heard the sounds of her friends being similarly roused, though, so she climbed out of bed and dressed hurriedly. She'd showered the night before, knowing from hard experience that any time she could grab a shower she had better avail herself of it, because it might be the last for a while. It meant sleeping with wet hair—and lots of it, given the length of Kerry's dark tresses. But that was a small price to pay for the pleasure of being able to stand her own company all day.

Even moving as quickly as she could, by the time she made it out, Season had put together one of her signature breakfast feasts. Kerry was a little too sleepy to take full advantage, but she managed an English muffin, a couple of cups of strong black tea, and a slice of bacon. Scott Banner filled his plate with a little of everything—scrambled eggs, hash browns, fruit, two kinds of toast, and bacon.

Brandy Pearson looked at his plate and snorted. "You have eaten before, right?" she prodded.

"Let him indulge," Season said. "We're not taking it with us, and I won't be coming back here again for a good long time, if ever. Might as well not waste it."

Scott simply nodded at Season's defense and shoveled another forkful of eggs into his mouth. He'd put on a bulky wool sweater with black jeans and the all-weather hiking boots he had been wearing the day before. Kerry thought he had put on a few pounds since summer, when they had all shared a house together in La Jolla, California. The weight looked good on him, filling out his gaunt cheeks a bit.

Rebecca Levine had taken too many off, and Kerry was still worried about her. She had hoped the redheaded free spirit would stay down in New York—or better yet, back in school at Santa Cruz—and far away from Season and the whole long-unresolved conflict. But here she was, too bighearted to let her friends face danger without being there too.

Brandy was the one Kerry had gone the longest without seeing. Her thick black hair was tied down with a red scarf, and her off-white sweater beautifully complemented her cocoa skin. Brandy had always been a girl who could put herself together, even when trouble was brewing. She shrugged off Season's defense of Scott and took another bite of the honeydew that, along with a cup of coffee, seemed to comprise her entire breakfast.

"You said before that we have to leave here," Brandy observed. "I get that. But where are we going? If Mother Blessing could track you guys down here, where will we be safe?"

Season set down her own coffee mug and regarded Brandy calmly. "I wish I had an answer for that," she said. "The truth is, I don't know. I can only strategize, but I have no guarantees."

"Okay, what's your strategy?" Rebecca asked.

"Here's what I've been thinking," Season replied. "We need to split up. Together, we'll be far too easy to find now that she has a line on all of us. Without you, Kerry, or her sons, she has no champions left, but she still has power, and even though we can beat her simulacra, there's still the chance that they could catch us by surprise. Or she could join the fight herself. I can beat Mother Blessing in a fair fight on neutral ground, I'm sure. But I don't think a fair fight is what she has in mind."

"So we all have to go different places?" Rebecca asked. The idea obviously caused her concern, and she didn't get her hands into her lap quick enough to hide their quaking from Kerry.

"For the most part," Season said, "I think you should all go back home. You back to Santa Cruz, Scott and Brandy back to Boston.

Resume your normal lives and activities, as much as possible. That way even if she does locate you again, there won't be any advantage to her to harass you, because you'll be out of it."

"Will we?" Scott asked. "Because I'm getting the distinct impression that this whole deal is kind of like the mob, or the CIA. Once you're in you can never really get out."

Season's nod was barely perceptible, but it was there. "There's some truth to that, Scott. I won't lie and say that you'll be completely safe. It depends partly on Mother Blessing. But if she observes you and understands that you're not in contact with me, that you're just going about your lives, then your chances are that much better. If we all stayed together, then you'd always be in jeopardy."

"Who is this 'we,' then?" Brandy wanted to know. "I notice you didn't say anything about Kerry going home."

"Maybe that's because I don't have one anymore," Kerry pointed out.

"Kerry is in this much more deeply than the rest of you," Season said. "She's a witch, Mother Blessing knows her well, and she's a target. She's probably in more danger because, skilled as she is, she still has a long way to go. If Mother Blessing really came at her, Kerry couldn't win. She needs to stay with me, for her own protection and training." Season paused, making eye contact with Kerry. "Does that sound okay to you, Kerry?"

If she had been asked even twelve hours earlier, Kerry would have hesitated. She hadn't decided quite how she felt about Season. The witch had, after all, killed Daniel, who was the only man Kerry had ever loved. And she had no real proof of her contention that it was Mother Blessing, and not herself, who was behind the slaughter in Slocumb. Her story rang truer than Mother Blessing's did, but Kerry was no expert lie detector. It was one witch's word against another's.

So she couldn't have said exactly why, but she agreed almost immediately. "Sure," she said. "I've got nowhere better to go, right?"

"That's one way to look at it."

Kerry knew there were several other ways to look at it too, but they all added up to the same response. She really was running out of other options. She had made a powerful enemy in Mother Blessing. She had left her Aunt

Betty and Uncle Marsh behind too many times, and wasn't so sure she'd be welcome back there. Her parents were dead, and her best friends in the world were the people in this room with her—the only people who could ever really know what she had been through since August.

And she figured Season was right in her evaluation of Kerry's abilities. She could do more witchy stuff than she'd been able to a few months before, but that probably meant she was just powerful enough to harm herself and others. She still needed tutelage, a mentor, and if Season wanted to be that, Kerry was happy to avail herself of the opportunity.

"Okay, then," she said cheerily. "I guess you're stuck with me."

Brandy eyed them both suspiciously. "But where are you guys going?" she inquired.

"I think it's best not to tell you," Season replied. "Not because we don't trust you— clearly, Kerry trusts you with her life, and that's good enough for me. But the fewer people who know, the safer everyone is."

"I don't like it at all," Brandy said. "But I guess I see your point."

"I'll be in touch as often as I can," Kerry promised. "So you guys don't have to worry about me."

"I'll still worry," Scott said.

Brandy nodded. "Don't take away Scott's favorite leisure-time activity. He's a gold medalist when it comes to worrying about you."

"I'm fine," Kerry stated flatly. "I've been in a couple of tight spots, but I've always come out okay. You don't need to worry about me, Scott. Especially if I'm with Season."

"I know," Scott said, blinking behind his glasses. "I mean, I understand that, intellectually. But it's not so easy when I don't know where you are or what you're doing. I always find myself thinking about the worst thing that could be happening, and assuming that *is* what's happening."

Rebecca laughed, covering her mouth with one hand. "But the truth is that whatever is really happening is usually even *worse* than Scott's imagination."

"Look, you guys." Kerry really hoped that she could persuade them of her safety, just as she had convinced them last night that she hadn't turned traitor or fallen under some kind of evil mind-control power of Season's. She knew what she was doing—okay, maybe that was a stretch. But she had some sense that she was doing the best thing for herself. These days—since the night she had met Daniel Blessing, really, changing her life forever—that was the most she could ask for. "I know I've said this before, but I really need you all to support me in this. And that means not worrying too much about me. You've all got your own lives to live, and I have mine. Mine is taking me in some directions that I didn't expect—but I think everyone probably finds out that's true, at some point or other. I mean, did your parents grow up thinking that they'd be pharmacists or lawyers or whatever? So I'm not taking the usual path. But I'm taking my own path, and you're taking yours, and we all just have to have some faith in one another's decision making."

Brandy snorted. "She's talking to you, Scott."

Kerry couldn't suppress a grin. "Thanks for not taking me seriously, Brandy," she said. "I could hardly believe that was me talking."

"It was a little drippy," Rebecca agreed. "But still—it made sense."

"Rebecca's right," Scott put in. "I don't mean to freak you out or anything, Kerry. I guess I'm just a worrywart by nature. But I do respect your decisions. If you and Season think you'll be safer, then Brandy and I will just go home and let you guys go wherever."

Season had been silent for a long time, just listening and letting the four friends work out their issues. Now she broke her silence. "I do think that's for the best," she said.

Kerry was glad the conversation had gone her way. "Sounds like it to me, too."

Scott looked at Brandy. "You need a ride, lady?"

"I guess I'm going your way," Brandy said. "If you think you have room for me."

"There's always room for you, Brandy," Scott said. "If you don't mind the stink of that mud man we had in the back seat."

Brandy looked as if she was thinking it over. "I guess I can put up with it as far as Boston," she admitted. "If we can stop at a car wash on the way. But we should probably be hitting the road—I'll have a lot of explaining to do when we get there."

Kerry was sorry their reunion had been so brief. One of these days, she wanted time to really catch up with her friends, to find out what was going on in their lives instead of just telling them what was up in hers. This wasn't going to be that time, though. Season was right—the sooner they vacated this cabin, the safer they'd all be.

2

"I've been doing some thinking," Rebecca said on the way to the airport in Burlington, Vermont, the nearest city with what passed for a "major" airport. "You guys should fly to California with me."

"That doesn't really help with the splitting up thing," Kerry answered. She guessed that Rebecca just really didn't want to be left alone again—even with her hardly-there roommate Erin. "Anyway, aren't you going back to New York, to spend the rest of the holidays with your folks?"

"I don't want to put them in any danger," Rebecca explained. "And anyway, I don't think I'd ever really feel safe there. California is about as far away from Mother Blessing as I can get, and Manhattan is so crowded that I'd never know who was real and who was one of her simulacra. In Santa Cruz you see the same familiar faces every day, and I'm more comfortable there.

"Anyway," she went on, "I wasn't thinking that you'd go to Santa Cruz with me. California is a huge state. I have these friends who own property up in Bolinas, on the coast up above San Francisco. They get tourists, but mostly it's this really out-of-the-way place where people value their privacy. Half the people up there are old-time hippies, and the rest are artists or hermits of one kind or another. There are a lot of marijuana farmers, too. They tend to be a suspicious bunch and don't like outsiders nosing around much. If you were there, I think you'd be pretty safe from Mother Blessing's minions."

"But we'd be outsiders too," Kerry said. She rode shotgun, and Rebecca sat in the back of Season's Jeep, which they would abandon at the airport. Kerry wondered momentarily how many vehicles Season had left behind in her life. Enough to fill a stadium parking lot, probably.

"Yeah, but you'd have someplace to be, so it would be okay."

"If we had the permission of your friends to use their place," Season added. "But getting that permission might endanger them."

"I'm sure I could swing that without telling them what it's for," Rebecca said. "That privacy thing cuts both ways. People who don't want others knowing their business are usually happy not to know yours."

"Sounds like it's worth checking out," Kerry suggested. "Unless you already have someplace in mind, Season."

Season glanced over at her and smiled, then faced the road once more. "I like it precisely because it's something I wouldn't have thought of," she said. "It's good to break out of old patterns if you're hiding from someone who knows you well. I'm pretty sure Mother Blessing is aware of most of my tricks by now."

"I'll call them," Rebecca said. "And when we get to the airport we can all fly together to San Francisco. From there I can get a shuttle to Santa Cruz, and you guys can rent a car or something to head up to Bolinas." Kerry heard a rustling as Rebecca dug out her cell phone and then dialed it. Kerry only half paid attention as Rebecca worked on persuading her friends, the Morgans, to let Season and Kerry use their place.

She realized she was happy to be on the move again. Since August she had spent a fair bit of time on the road, running toward or away from one witch or another. Rootless, her only permanent home now had a white line running down its middle—either that or two wings and jet engines that lifted her far above the Earth. Motion was the only constant, staying in one place too long the greatest danger. This had been Season's reality for centuries, and now it was also Kerry's. She wasn't sure if she truly liked it, but she was getting used to it.

If nothing else, she had learned the virtue of flexibility.

Scott pulled his RAV4 away from the curb after dropping Brandy at her parents' home in Needham, where she had wanted to go instead of back to her own apartment. He had wanted to be invited in. Even though he was a little nervous about seeing her brothers, afraid they blamed him for their breakup and maybe for her missing Christmas, he liked her family and missed spending time with them. She didn't extend that invitation, though. They had chatted amicably enough on the drive down from New Hampshire, with Brandy slipping in the occasional stinging barb, as she had a habit of doing. But she had grown quieter as they closed on the Boston area, her mood almost visibly darkening. He knew she was worried about Adam Castle, her new boyfriend, and about facing her family after skipping out on them at Christmas. At the end of the trip, she quietly thanked him for the ride and gave him a perfunctory hug.

Scott was still not thrilled with the idea that Brandy had a new boyfriend, but he was trying to adjust. He and Brandy had been a good thing for a long time, but that was over. He and Kerry could be a good thing too, he was sure, but it was looking like that would never happen. He glanced in his rearview mirror as he drove away from her block, watching it recede behind him like some kind of suburban metaphor for the longest romantic relationship of his life.

He knew he would still see Brandy from time to time, no matter what. Kerry too—or at least he devoutly hoped so. She would be farther away, however, and he would continue to worry about her, no matter what she wanted. Season would be a better ally for her than he could ever be, but he nonetheless felt better when she was someplace where he could keep an eye on her. Now she was no doubt winging or riding somewhere halfway across the continent, and he was back in the position of having to wait for her to get in touch with him whenever the mood struck her.

As he turned the corner he stole one last glance at Brandy's house. But in his mind's eye he could see Kerry's slow but genuine smile, her green eyes flashing like twin emeralds catching the sun, her long black hair falling over her face and then being swept away, and he knew that such a beautiful vision would never leave him, no matter what else happened in his life.

The San Francisco airport was a terrible place for good-byes. It was crowded and busy, with travelers bustling in every direction, all pulling wheeled suitcases as if they were oversized, blocky dogs, with security people, flight attendants, pilots and staff, and families waiting for or dropping off their loved ones. It meant there was no real privacy, no place for the kind of conversation Rebecca, Season, and Kerry really needed to have.

Instead of trying to talk in detail, they resorted to a kind of code. "So," Rebecca said. "You have my number. If you need anything, just call. Otherwise, my friends are expecting you to be at their place. If it goes more than a couple of months, it wouldn't hurt to call up, but I don't think they're planning on being back up there until early summer. I told you where the key is, right?"

"Yes," Season said. "We know where to look for it."

"And you have my cell, right?" Kerry asked redundantly, knowing full well that Rebecca did. What she didn't know was whether she'd have coverage in Bolinas—it sounded pretty rural, the way Rebecca described it. But she had also said it was a tourist destination, so maybe her phone would work fine. At the very worst, she could always augment it magically, as Mother Blessing had done with her laptop in the Great Dismal Swamp. "If you see or hear any signs of her, you let us know, okay? Don't take any chances with her." Obviously, everyone knew who the "her" referred to.

"Hello," Rebecca said. "Do you know me? Do you remember me being someone who takes chances?"

"You've taken a lot of them, Beck," Kerry said. "I just want you to be safe, okay?"

"That's what I want too," Rebecca assured her. "Well, for both of us—all of us—to be safe."

"The sooner we split up the safer we'll be," Season said. She scanned the crowds like a wary hawk. "I'm sorry, I'm not trying to rush you, Rebecca, but we really need to get going."

"I know," Rebecca said. "It'll be late by the time I get home too. I just . . . I don't want you guys to go."

"I don't either, Beck," Kerry said, suddenly sorry for her friend. Of all her summer friends, Rebecca might have been the least capable of dealing with the kinds of things they had learned—the existence of real witches, the magic, the constant danger. Kerry knew that going back to college in Santa Cruz, living in that big, ramshackle house with Erin, and being so far from the others was going to be tougher on her than on anyone else. She wished there was something she could do to make it easier.

But there wasn't. Inviting Rebecca to stay with them up in Bolinas would just expose her to even more potential danger. Season was right—Rebecca was safest living her own normal life, far away from them. She wouldn't like it, at least at first, but it was for the best.

Kerry wrapped her arms around her friend and gave her a firm squeeze. Rebecca returned it, sniffling a little as she did. *No tears,* Kerry mentally pleaded. *I don't know if I can take it.*

When she pulled away, there was moisture in Rebecca's eyes, but none escaped. Kerry blinked back a little of her own, and then Rebecca turned away and headed for the shuttles. Kerry and Season stood there for a few minutes, until Rebecca was out of sight. Then Kerry turned to the older woman.

"What now? We can't take a cab to Bolinas, right?"

"For tonight?" Season asked, almost incredulous. "We're in San Francisco, girl. Let's get a hotel room and do it right."

As it happens, Season's idea of doing it right was not precisely the same as mine would have been. Not that I'm club-girl or anything. But a little shopping might have been fun. It was pretty late at night by the time we were checked in at the Mark Hopkins, but still, big city, right? Something must have been open.

Instead, Season got us a cab and went into North Beach, where she took me to a hole-in-the-wall Italian restaurant that I never would have looked twice at. Once I was inside, though, it was like Pavlov's dog all over again—the aroma was heavenly and I was suddenly so famished it was like I had never eaten the cardboard baguette sandwich they served on the plane. Which, in fact, I hadn't, because you know, cardboard.

I just let her order, because the whole menu was in Italian and I was too hungry to even read English. I won't try to re-create the dinner here—let's just say that everything I ate was so good that my mouth thought it had died and gone to heaven, leaving the rest of me earthbound. The staff treated us both like old friends, although Season swore that's just the way they are, and she had never seen any of them before.

After dinner we walked around North Beach for a

while, just watching the people, tourists and locals alike. It's quite a show. We chatted about the people we saw and the weather—cool, but nothing like Chicago or New Hampshire, with a fog that eventually rolled in off the bay like someone pulling a blanket over a bed. Basically, we covered everything except Mother Blessing and what lay ahead of us.

Which was fine. I dwell on that stuff enough as it is. It was good to have my attention distracted by something else for a bit.

I almost typed "for a spell" but decided that would be just too witchy of me. Witchy and old-fashioned, which kind of go together, considering that other than me, the youngest witch I know is, like, three hundred and some years older than I am.

Now we're back in the room—*très luxe!*—and Season's getting ready for bed while I do the dear diary thing. But she'll come out soon and then it's my turn, and then another early start in the morning. I'm a little trepidatious, I admit, about what tomorrow holds, and the day after that, and so on. Me and Season Howe, teamed up? Who'd have ever thought?

More later.

K.

"I'll be Margaret Thurston," Season said. "And you're my niece, Melissa King."

They were in the back of a taxi, bouncing over San Francisco's famous hills on the way to a used car lot Season had found listed in the hotel room's phone book.

"But you'll have to show some identification to buy a car, right?" Kerry asked. "I did, when I bought that van to go down to the Great Dismal."

Season just looked at her, smiling. It took Kerry a few seconds to realize her mistake.

"Oh," she said when she caught on.

To demonstrate, Season opened her wallet and handed it over. Inside it, every identifying item showed the name Margaret Thurston: a valid California driver's license with a Bay Area address, several credit cards, a Social Security card, even a library card. A checkbook had the same name, with a local address imprinted on the checks. "And mine all say Melissa King, right?"

"That's right."

Kerry double-checked the window between the front and back seats. It was mostly closed, but there was a narrow gap through which passengers could speak to the driver. The driver had her radio on, though, playing loud reggae music, so Kerry figured as long as they spoke in low tones they wouldn't be overheard.

"So on top of everything else, you could be a world-class counterfeiter," Kerry said. "Do you manufacture your own money, too?"

"I don't," Season answered. Under a tan leather jacket, she wore a snug blue turtleneck that was almost as vibrant as her piercing blue eyes, with faded brown jeans and black boots, and her blond hair hung loose, framing her face. "I know I wouldn't ever make so much of it that I'd have a real impact on the national economy, but the possibility exists—a witch could manufacture so much cash, and flood the markets with it, that it could devalue our currency. Because I want to make sure that never happens I only spend money that I earn."

"But you don't have a job," Kerry pointed out.

"Maybe 'earn' isn't the right word," Season admitted. "I have investments, under various names. I gamble sometimes, although I try to resist the temptation to push the odds in my favor. I have a bank account in most cities, collecting interest. Every few years I move them around, because an account in constant use for a hundred years might raise some eyebrows. One of those accounts is here in the Bay Area, under the name Margaret Thurston. I have as much as I need, especially since I make a lot of my own clothing and food."

Kerry thought of her own bank account, established with money from an insurance settlement after her mother's death. She had tapped it a few times since summer, never putting anything back in. There were still several thousand dollars in it, but if she continued on as she had been it wouldn't last a whole lot longer. Would she follow in Season's footsteps, constantly on the move and making witchery her lifelong career? Or was this just another phase in her life that she'd pass through in a little while? She had a hard time picturing herself doing anything more mundane after this experience. Working a food service job or being stuck inside an office seemed like they'd be claustrophobic at best. And her experience with higher education—vanishing from Northwestern a few weeks into her first term—was not promising so far.

She wanted to talk to Season about it, to find out more about her early life and how she had made the decision to be a witch—if there were even any other options open to her—but the cab pulled to the curb beside a sprawling car lot, decorated with multicolored pennants on ropes and sporting dozens of gleaming, polished vehicles. "Here you go, ladies," the driver said through the window. Season pushed a twenty through the window at her, and the two witches stepped out onto the sidewalk.

"Let me do the talking," Season said. "The van you bought was okay for you, but I think we're going to want four-wheel drive up in the country. And you never pay sticker at a place like this."

Another vital life lesson from Season Howe, Kerry thought as a salesman approached. He grinned like a hungry shark, and Kerry realized she was happy to let Season handle the negotiation.

3

An hour later they were crossing the rust-red span of the Golden Gate Bridge, heading north out of the city. Bolinas wasn't far up the coast, but it sat on the end of a little spur of land, separated from the rest of the state by the Point Reyes National Seashore. That isolated it enough that the locals felt they had their much-sought-after privacy.

Through a spattering rain, Season drove the old silver Dodge Raider they'd settled on, up Highway One through affluent Marin County. They made one stop, at a supermarket where they laid in some provisions—"real food," Kerry called it, as opposed to the magically created kind.

As they neared Point Reyes the rain picked up, a solid curtain of it through which visibility was almost nonexistent. Heading into the park, sheets of water filled the narrow roadways. Kerry noticed that Season's knuckles were white on the wheel, and her easy chatter of earlier in the drive had died. All her focus was on the task of negotiating the road. The beauty of Point Reyes was unmistakable, but Kerry could barely see it, and she knew that Season was missing it altogether. She hoped they'd have a chance to come back sometime, to explore the oddly twisted pines and the wind-and-water-sculpted cliffs.

Instead of letting up as they progressed, the storm just dumped ever more rain on them—glimpses of the ocean were redundant, as there seemed to be as much water falling from the sky as in the Pacific. A few cars passed them, their occupants looking like tourists distressed that their trip to Stinson Beach had been ruined by the downpour. But they soon turned off the main road onto an old country lane that led away from Bolinas's minimal "downtown" and through rolling, grassy hills.

The storm let up a little, and Kerry noticed that Season visibly relaxed now that she was off the main road. So she decided to bring up a question that had been on her mind for a long time—one of those that she thought of, then forgot to ask, on a regular basis, usually remembering again at only the most inopportune moments.

"Season, that storm, when you attacked Mother Blessing's place in the Swamp—did you cause that? Or was it one of her defenses? Or just a natural occurrence?"

Season glanced at her. "I guess this is as good a time as any to bring up something I wanted to talk about," she said, apparently ignoring Kerry's question altogether.

"What?"

"I've offered to teach you, to help you develop your obviously significant gifts. And for the last few days, I've pretty much been willing to answer any question you threw my way. But once we get settled into our new place, we'll be going back to a routine like we had at Christmas."

"The no-more-than-ten-questions thing? Why?"

"We might change the number—maybe fifteen per day, or something like that, since we'll be working closely together. But the reason we'll be working together is so you can learn. To do that, you have to be focused. Asking a million questions about any trivial matter that pops into your head is a scattershot way of learning, and it's not that effective. If you have to think your questions through, really narrow down what you need to know and sift out those things you can figure out on your own, then you'll learn much more quickly, and you'll retain more."

"I guess that makes sense," Kerry admitted. She felt a little thwarted by the idea, although Season's reasoning seemed sound. "But you said that starts when we get settled?"

"Right."

"Which means I can ask questions now, right?"

"Uh-huh," Season answered. Most of her attention was still on the road, keeping the vehicle in contact with the wet pavement and trying to follow the directions they'd been given.

"So why are you doing this? Why take me under your wing like this? What's in it for you?"

Season hazarded another, longer glance at

Kerry before facing front again. "I thought it was obvious," she said. "Like I told you, you are a gifted witch. A kind of diamond in the rough, I suppose. But anyone who learned as much as you in those few weeks with Mother Blessing is a person to be reckoned with."

Kerry thought her heart would burst with pride at that description. She wasn't sure she could live up to it, but she would definitely try.

"Part of being a witch is giving back to the community of witches," Season went on. "One way to do that is to help teach and develop young witches, so that the traditions are carried on. In this case, of course, there's also a much more practical consideration."

"What's that?"

"Mother Blessing and I have been at each other's throats for centuries," Season explained. "We've each won some battles, but the overall war goes on. One of these days, one of us is going to have to prevail. I would much rather have you on my side in the conflict than hers, because frankly, I could use some allies here."

Kerry started to say that she was honored that Season would consider her aid anything to be desired, but as she was composing her thoughts, Season interrupted. "And that storm in the Great Dismal, by the way, was mine. Mother Blessing knew I was coming, but I was hoping to mask my exact progress to some extent, so she wouldn't know precisely where I was or when I'd reach her home."

"It worked," Kerry said. "She was trying to prepare, but you caught her before she was completely ready."

"And still, I couldn't beat her," Season recalled. "Partly because she is most powerful on her home ground, where she has lived for so long. And partly because she had your help."

"Did I really make that big a difference?" Kerry asked, surprised.

"Do you really have to ask?"

Before Kerry could answer the question, Season pulled off the little country lane onto a rutted dirt track, just the width of two sets of wheels. "Here we are," she said, ticking her head toward a mailbox with a street number painted on it.

The track wound between spreading oaks, down into a little incline where a wood-sided house stood. It was a single story, with a porch across the front. Its blue paint, faded, blistered, and peeling from the sun and weather, was rain-darkened, and water dripped from its eaves. The roof had seen better days, but Kerry figured if it was dry inside, after the storm that had blown through today, then it would hold up fine.

Season parked at the end of the drive, in a little dirt circle right before the front door. "Home again, home again," she said.

They had left New Hampshire with very little. Kerry brought her usual duffel containing a few changes of clothes, some of Daniel's journals, and her laptop computer. Season had a leather backpack that seemed to contain anything she would ever need. Kerry was convinced that if she ever looked inside, it would be empty, and that Season just conjured what she wanted from it. They hauled the groceries inside and dumped the bags on a table made from raw oak planks, sanded but not sealed or painted. The kitchen was small, but clean water ran from the tap, the refrigerator was cold, and the gas oven and stove seemed to work. The owners had an interesting sense of color—the kitchen's walls were fire-engine red and bright blue, while the floor was yellow and the appliances white and gold.

The rest of the house echoed the general color chaos. Wooden walls were painted in seemingly whatever color had struck someone's fancy at a given moment, or maybe just in whatever was on sale at the hardware store. Most of the floors were unpainted, but there were exceptions, including a forest green one with red polka dots.

There seemed to be a great deal of wildlife—spiders, ants, flies, and other less immediately identifiable creepy-crawlies—inside the house that Kerry would just as soon have had living outside instead. She figured that it was a function of the house having been unoccupied for a stretch, and that once she and Season had made the place their own, the bugs would move out. Living in the swamp had given her a greater tolerance for insect life than she'd ever had before, and learning witchcraft had impressed on her the role that all living things played in the world. Mother Blessing had told her it was scientific fact that if all the insects in the world were to suddenly vanish, all other life on the planet would end within two weeks. Mother Blessing had made a lot of outrageous claims, but Kerry couldn't help suspecting there was some truth to that one.

In spite of the colors and the creatures, the house was cozy and plenty comfortable enough for Kerry's liking. The furniture was old, mismatched, and lived in, as if it had grown up organically within the house. A door led from the kitchen into a small grassy back-yard with a few rows of herbs and vegetables, overgrown now but offering the promise of fresh food with only a little work and atten-tion. Beyond that were woods that seemed to go on forever. The room Kerry chose as her bedroom was next to the only bathroom, and though it was a little smaller than the other bedroom, it had a built-in window seat where she could already imagine herself reading and writing at night.

In the middle of the afternoon, after Kerry had hung up her clothes in the room's tiny closet and shoved some furniture around so she'd be able to see trees out the window from her bed, Season called her into the kitchen. Two cups of hot tea and a plate of cookies were set out on the table. Season sat in one of the four random chairs that surrounded it, looking expectantly at Kerry. It was clear that she'd been summoned for a particular reason, so Kerry took a chair and drew one of the cups to her. She wasn't going to waste one of her questions by asking what was up.

"I wanted to tell you what is really going on here," Season said after a moment. "Why Mother Blessing has stepped up the pace of attacks against me, and why staying with me puts you in considerable danger."

"Okay." Outside, the rain continued to beat down on the roof, creating a kind of staccato background music for their conversation.

"You know about the Witches' Convocation," Season declared plainly. "It starts on the first day of spring. One of the important functions of the Convocation is to rule on disputes between witches, as well as on crimes against witchcraft and crimes by witches against humanity. We firmly believe in policing ourselves, so that the outside world never decides it has to take action against us."

"Which means that the Convocation will finally address what happened in Slocumb," Kerry said, careful in her phrasing. She was determined to save her questions.

"That's right," Season agreed. "We have a

very rigid and highly developed system of justice, which is prepared to deal with all of those issues I just described. The Slocumb incident will definitely have a hearing in Witches' Tribunal. Mother Blessing has been spreading her version of things ever since it happened, and even though her version is a lie, there's a little bit of that 'common knowledge' thing operating in her favor."

"People tend to believe something they've heard over and over, even if there's no truth to it," Kerry stated.

"Exactly. I've tried to get my story out there too, but it's been harder for me. For one thing, I didn't know she was spreading her tales for a long time, until they started filtering back to me. And then, she had me on the run for so long that it was hard to get a fair hearing—I looked guilty simply because I wasn't sitting still and waiting for her to finish me off."

"That's not fair."

"That's true. But then, fairness is what the Convocation is for. I'll be at a disadvantage because so many will have heard Mother Blessing's side of it, but the hearing will be as impartial as possible. Which is why Mother

Blessing would love to get rid of me before it happens. She could use the Slocumb incident as a defense when the hearing about my death came up, as it certainly would. But that would be an easier sell for her, since she wouldn't have to worry about my testimony contradicting hers."

"So she'd like to kill you before it starts, but even if she doesn't, she stands a good chance of beating you in court?"

"That about sums it up," Season admitted sadly. "She isn't guaranteed to win. I happen to believe that the truth will sway the Tribunal to my side. And I think there's a way to prove that truth. But I'm going to need your help."

"My help?"

"That's right. I need someone I can trust completely, someone familiar with the facts, and someone who is very powerful and skilled."

"But I have a long way to go before I'm those things."

"And it's not quite January," Season replied. "Which is why we need to train so hard between now and the Convocation. I'm going to want you by my side, Kerry. More than that. I'm going to need you. Will you be there for me?"

Stunned that she was being asked, being trusted with so much, at first it was all Kerry could do to nod her head. "Of course," she said finally. "I'll do whatever I can."

"That's good," Season said, a warm smile spreading over her face. "That's the best I can ask for."

4

Mother Blessing wheeled angrily around her home in the Great Dismal Swamp, her motorized scooter's rubber tires squeaking on the hardwood floors. Somehow Season Howe had survived her onslaught. It had taken every ounce of strength Mother Blessing could bring to bear to create nearly a hundred simulacra, and still the witch had defeated them. If only she had been able to manifest them all at once instead of one at a time, however quickly. That might have proven too much even for someone of Season's abilities.

But that great an effort, over such a distance, was beyond her. She had lain for days in her bed after the post-Christmas assault, exhausted by her efforts. It was only now, a couple of days after the passing of the year, that she was able to get around again. The immediate aftereffects of her spell had passed, but the fury hadn't.

Allowing Kerry Profitt to receive communications while she was here in this house had been a stroke of genius. Doing so had enabled Mother Blessing to learn who was close to Kerry, who might be keeping tabs on her whereabouts. So when the urgent call had passed from one to the next—*We've found Season!*—Mother Blessing had known approximately where to begin looking. By watching through the eyes of her simulacrum scouts, she had spotted the young interlopers, and they had led her right to Kerry and Season.

It only added to her rage that Kerry and Season seemed to have teamed up. She had groomed Kerry to be an arrow that she could let fly at Season at any time. For that weapon to be turned so quickly against her was nothing short of infuriating.

But there was no one in the house to shout at, no one to complain to or abuse. So she slammed doors and made sharp turns with her scooter, envisioning the faces of her enemies on the floor and wishing she could roll over them as easily.

A new year had begun. The Convocation would be upon her in a matter of weeks. There was a chance that she would prevail in the Witches' Tribunal, but there was also always a chance that she would not. Far better to finally get Season out of the way before then.

And she could do it, she was convinced. Her mistake had always been in sending others to do the job. Her sons had turned out to be weak—not ruthless enough, or possibly not determined enough. She didn't know what the problem was, but they obviously had some failing that she had not recognized before. Kerry Profitt might have been forged into a useful weapon, given time, but she had been young, inexperienced, and Season had come before Mother Blessing had had a chance to finish with her.

So the task fell to her. Had she recognized this fact years ago, perhaps this war would have been long since over. She had always thought there was time, plenty of time. But suddenly the Convocation loomed. If it had been an annual event, or even a centennial one, perhaps she'd have been better prepared for it. Over the course of five hundred years, though—and this being the first and possibly the only one of her lifetime—it had kind of crept up on her.

It would take her awhile to be ready for another battle. Weeks, maybe. Months would be better, but she didn't have months. Any moves against Season this close to the Convocation would automatically be suspect.

On the other hand, Season's presence at the Witches' Tribunal would be more perilous still.

She would just have to make sure that Season didn't show up for the Witches' Convocation. No matter what it took.

Dawn hadn't even cracked, if that's what dawn really did, when Kerry rolled out of bed at Season's summons. For the last several weeks, Season had been running her ragged. Up at first light, warming up, performing calisthenics in the cold morning air. Then a long run, at least five miles, before breakfast. Kerry kept thinking she'd get used to it, but so far she hadn't. Every night she went to bed with muscles sore from the day's workout, and every morning she woke up with aches worse than she'd had the night before.

After the run and a big breakfast, she and Season went out into the fields, forests, and beaches of the area for nature lessons. This area wasn't as rich in biological diversity as the Great Dismal Swamp had been, but it was still abundant in its plant species, and only slightly less so in animal life. And as Season explained, variety wasn't an absolute necessity—more important was the practitioner's connection with the natural forces that flowed through those plants and animals. Kerry, Season noted, had an almost innate ability to make that connection.

She could sit in the middle of a meadow with the wind pushing the tall grasses toward her, and the susurrus of the grass seemed to be a private conversation that only Kerry could understand. She could wait patiently with her arms extended in a forest glade, and birds would drop down to her hands. She had to overcome her distaste for insects, but once she had, they would crawl up her arms and legs without stinging, biting, or otherwise molesting her. Even the enormous elephant seals on the beach at Point Reyes responded to her. She made eye contact with one, which then rolled over onto its back, flippers extended out toward her, and uttered three long, deep-throated squeals in her direction.

After time spent communing with nature, the daily schedule called for a reading period. Kerry knew that Season had not brought an entire library's worth of magical texts with her to the Bolinas house, but the books were there, and Season assigned a heavy study regimen. These books reinforced what Mother Blessing and Season had taught her, but went into considerably greater detail about the origins of witchcraft, the theory behind individual spells, and even some of the great witches of the past.

The reading period was followed by lunch, and then by one-on-one instruction from Season, putting some of the things she had read into practical use. This usually took most of the afternoon, but if there was time, Season put her through more physical training.

"Stamina is just as important as knowing the ancient words of power backward and forward," Season explained on one of the many occasions when Kerry complained about the hard workouts. After dinner they sat around together, making small talk or discussing the events of the day. "It does you absolutely no good to know the words you say if you don't have the strength to put behind the spells. And if the first couple of spells knock you on your tail, you won't be around long enough to become an experienced witch."

"Yeah, but if the workout kills me, what good does all the knowledge do?"

"People almost always survive exercise," Season answered with a smile.

"And if I'd wanted to join the Marines, I would have."

"Are you calling me a drill sergeant, Private Profitt?"

"Hey, if the combat boot fits . . ."

The thing was, Kerry believed it was working. She had been in the best shape of her life when she'd been in the Swamp with Mother Blessing, but now, after just a few weeks with Season, she was even stronger. Her stomach was flat, her thighs and calves hard and sinewy, her arms and shoulders rippling with muscle. The old "no pain, no gain" saying seemed to have a lot of truth to it. Kerry definitely had the pain, but the gain was also unmistakable.

And the changes weren't confined to the physical. Kerry realized that she was sleeping more soundly—and falling asleep earlier, thanks to the way too early wake-up call—and her mood was generally positive and upbeat.

In this way the days sped by quickly—days of wind and weather, of frantic activity, of cramming her head so full of information that she was sure it would explode.

One night in late January, Season sat across from Kerry in the house's living room, crowded with a sofa, several chairs, and an assortment of tables that looked like they'd been purchased at flea markets over the years. Outside, yet another winter storm battered the roof. Season looked cozy in a red polar fleece top and black corduroy jeans. Kerry had layered a couple of T-shirts together, and sitting near the fire she was perfectly comfortable in those and blue jeans.

"I've noticed something interesting these last couple of weeks," Season began. She had poured herself a cup of hot tea, and on the oak coffee table she placed a cardboard box full of herbs she and Kerry had collected early on and hung in the kitchen to dry, and an old stone mortar and pestle. Kerry put down the book she was reading—a thriller from the 1970s that she'd found on a shelf in the house, not one of the magical texts—and looked at Season.

"What is it?" she asked.

Season put some of the herbs into the mortar before she answered. "Teaching you, working with you, has had an unexpected benefit for me as well," she said.

Kerry waited for her to continue. Season had a habit of revealing things at her own pace, no matter what.

"I've been pretty consumed," Season went on finally, grinding away with the pestle, "with either running from, or battling, Mother Blessing and her minions. It's taken so much of my time and energy that there hasn't been much left for anything else. Watching you, trying to see the world—and witchcraft—through your eyes, I've remembered what drew me to witchcraft in the first place."

"You were drawn?" Kerry asked. "You weren't born into it?"

"My father was a witch," Season replied. "Not my mother. She wanted nothing to do with it, and in fact convinced him to renounce his gifts. Those were dangerous times for witches in Europe, so it was probably a good decision in terms of prolonging his life. But it meant that I had aunts and one surviving grandmother who could tell me stories about the craft and point me in the right direction when I had made up my mind."

"And when you did, obviously you decided to go the witchy route," Kerry observed.

"Not at first. But there weren't a lot of opportunities for women in those days. I could have worked as a scullery maid, or married, or joined a convent. None of those particularly suited me, even then. My father always tried to impress upon me that I was different, special somehow. I guess I believed him. And then I watched women all around me leading miserable lives but saw that my aunts and grandmother were not only healthy and well kept, but commanded respect in their villages. With those role models, I could hardly turn my back."

"So they fulfilled the mentor role for you . . ."

"That I am trying to do for you, Kerry. That's right. And by doing so, I've reconnected to some of that sense of discovery I felt in those days. Learning how the world really works, how everything is connected. Feeling the excitement of creating a spell and watching it come about. There's a thrill of creativity that happens, which I've kind of lost track of."

"I know what you mean," Kerry said. "I feel the same thing when one works just right."

"Watching you, seeing the spark in your eyes, that's what reminded me of it all. I'm indebted to you, Kerry. Thanks for showing it to me again."

Kerry was nonplussed—not for the first time since meeting Season. "I—I'm the one who should be indebted, Season," she stammered. "You could have killed me, or at least sent me back to Mother Blessing. But you agreed to take me on, just like that—I can still hardly believe my luck."

"I think you're failing to see the big picture, Kerry. It's not just you who needs me. We both need each other." She took the pestle out of the mortar, in which she had crushed the dried herbs to a fine powder. "Think about that, okay?"

Kerry Profitt's diary, January 24.

So Season owes me? The first impression test tells me that's crazy. So do the second and third. I owe her, huge. But what I've done *for* her could be measured in a teaspoon, I think. If you had a microscope to find it.

I mean, that whole thing she said earlier this evening about having connected somehow with the reasons she became a witch. A little touchy-feely, maybe, but still really sweet. And maybe there's even a modicum of truth to it—"modicum" being a word I was reacquainted with in one of Season's books, and I like it. It's kind of like forgetting how good popsicles taste on a hot day, and then you take a little kid to the store and buy him one, and you get your own, and when you lick it you remember why you liked them in the first place.

Or something like that. Only probably more profound.

But she told me to think about the fact that we both need each other, so that's what I've been doing. I can come up with plenty of reasons I need her: so I don't get killed, so I don't kill myself, so I can continue my training, so I can become the witch I'd like to be, etc. etc.

As for why she needs me . . . ? To help her battle Mother Blessing, I guess. And for whatever is coming at the Convocation, for which she told me she'll need my help. But I still don't know with what. The Convocation is a couple of months away, but getting closer all the time. Every now and then she drops hints about it, things she's heard over the years, and it sounds *amazing.* I can't wait to see it for myself.

I guess I have to, though. Wait, I mean.

What's it going to be like? Has a girl ever looked forward to something with such delirious anticipation?

Well, it so happens that I didn't go to my prom. I guess this is my consolation prize.

Although if you want the truth, this is about a million times cooler.

More later.

K.

5

Rebecca stood on the boardwalk, quiet this time of day. On a weekend, or later in the evening, it would be bustling with people playing for a chance at cheap prizes, lining up for the roller coaster, eating corn dogs and cotton candy. It was like a county fair or a circus all year long, except even more threadbare than most, with a sense of desperation underlying it, as if anyone who couldn't have fun here was just out of luck altogether.

Rebecca wasn't having any fun.

February had already bled into March. The school year was passing by, and she was attending class (well, most of the time—she should have been in class now, instead of at the beach) and trying to pay attention. Her grades had been passable, though not excellent. Nowhere near what she could have done if she had "applied herself"—a phrase Rebecca had heard many times during her school career—but at least she wasn't flunking out.

But although she got up every morning, ate a meal, went to school, did homework, read a little, the whole thing seemed like an exercise, a rehearsal for real life instead of life itself. She spent every day waiting for something that didn't come.

She knew what the problem was, of course, and it had more than one part. She lived on the edge of fear now, never knowing when Mother Blessing, or Season, or some other witch entirely might reenter her life. Death followed in the wake of witches, that was her experience. And she couldn't quite believe that witches were gone from her life. Kerry Profitt, after all, seemed well on her way to becoming one. And the last time she had talked to Kerry, a month or so before, they were still up in Bolinas at the Morgans' place, and Kerry seemed to be more excited by her new path than ever.

So that was the first part—one of these days, Kerry or one of the witches associated with her would show up, and her life would be spun topsy-turvy again.

The second part was the fear that the first part wouldn't happen after all.

Because now Rebecca knew what most people never did. She understood that there was another aspect to life. And while that aspect was often terrifying, it was also exciting. Even the terror made her feel more *alive* than anything else she had ever encountered. The whole thing—the thrill of the chase, the shiver of horror when she learned that something she had believed was nonsense, or legend at best, was true—she couldn't shake her hunger for it.

Is that why Kerry threw herself into it? Rebecca wondered as she stared off into the blue distance, looking at the line where sky met sea. *Is she addicted too?*

And can addictions ever be good for you?

It was one of those Boston days when people begin to believe that spring will come around again. The gutters ran with melting snow, which for at least a week had been dirty and blackened by exhaust and grime. Joggers ran along the banks of the Charles in shorts and

T-shirts instead of all bundled up in sweats. Light green leaves caught the brilliant sunlight, adding grace notes to branches that had been bare and gray for months.

Ordinarily Brandy would have loved being out on a day like this.

But not today.

Today Adam Castle had decided to pick a fight.

They had gone for a walk to enjoy the springlike weather. Brandy wore a light leather jacket over a cashmere sweater, with black pants and black flats. Adam had on blue jeans, white athletic shoes, and a navy Cambridge sweatshirt. Both had felt relieved at not having to put on a winter coat.

When they got back to his apartment, Adam stopped just inside the door and turned to Brandy. "I've been trying to figure out a way to say this for a long time," he said. "And I just can't think of anything except coming right out with it."

Brandy felt like she'd been sucker punched. She prided herself on being able to read people, but she hadn't known there was anything weighing on Adam beyond the usual work stuff. She closed the door gently behind herself. "With what? What's wrong, Adam?"

"It's . . . I feel like you don't trust me, Brandy. Like there's a whole huge part of your life you don't let me see. It's like you're one of those people who has a second family in a different city."

Now the sucker punch sensation turned into a twisting of her gut, because Adam had proven to be extraordinarily perceptive. He was exactly right. She had been keeping something from him—something huge. She felt like she couldn't explain about Season Howe and Mother Blessing and Kerry. So she had made up stories about her summer job in San Diego, and then others to explain things like her sudden trip to New Hampshire at Christmas. The lies she had fabricated then demanded other lies to support them, and she had found herself constructing a whole network of untruth.

Still, she had thought her psychological insight and studies had allowed her to pull it off. Now, learning that she hadn't, she felt terrible about the whole thing.

Just not terrible enough to confess, she thought. *Some things he really is best off not knowing.*

"I don't know what you mean, Adam," she said, after a hesitation that she recognized had stretched a little too long.

"Are you sure?" he pressed. "Do you really want me to run down the laundry list of little lies I've caught you in, or times you've evaded questions? Because I can, Brandy. I've dwelled on it long enough."

"That's not what I'm saying, Adam." She searched his face, dark and scowling, for any sign of the man she had come to care about so deeply. She couldn't yet bring herself to use the word "love," but the very fact that it floated at the edge of her consciousness meant something. At any rate, she enjoyed his company and didn't want to lose him.

"Then what?" he asked. "Either I'm right or I'm wrong."

"You're . . . you're wrong, then."

He flopped down on his couch, his hands folded into tight fists. "You're sure about that. You haven't been hiding anything from me. That trip out of town at Christmas, the one you took with your ex and came back from all exhausted and freaked out—you were visiting a sick friend? Come on, Brandy, that story's always been lame."

"That's not what I said, and you know it," Brandy objected.

"Sorry," Adam said with an angry sneer. "Not a sick friend. A friend in trouble. What kind of trouble you never told me, though."

"Because it was none of your business," Brandy fired back. "If she had wanted strangers to know her personal issues she would have said so. You don't know her, and you don't need to know what she was going through— you just need to know that she needed me, and that should be good enough for you."

"Should be," Adam said. "But it isn't. Not on top of everything else. I'm sorry, Brandy, but I can't be in a relationship with half of someone. If you can't open your whole life to me, then it's just not going to work."

"I . . . I've given you as much of myself as I can, Adam," Brandy said, aware that she was on the verge of sounding like she was pleading. She wouldn't go that far, though. Not for Adam or any other man. He was smart, funny, good-looking, and successful. A real prize. But not prize enough to humiliate herself over.

"That's not all of you, though." His eyes had been burning a hole through her, but now he went to the window and looked away, toward the far side of the river. "It's not enough."

"Adam, hasn't there ever been anything in your life that you just had to keep to yourself? Something that was maybe too private, or too dangerous, for other people to know?"

Adam let out a soft chuckle, but one with no humor in it. "What are you now, Brandy? Some kind of spy?"

"That's not what I'm trying to say, Adam."

"I wish you knew what you were trying to say, then, because it isn't working."

"But . . . Adam," Brandy said, bordering on desperation again. She couldn't tell him the truth, and he would have to live with that. "You've got to just understand on this one. You can't push it."

He spun around to face her again. "I *am* pushing it, Brandy. Consider yourself pushed. You've admitted that you've been lying, hiding things from me. That's what I needed to know. Now you have two options. You can either tell me the truth—all of it, from jump—or you can admit that your secrets are more important to you than I am."

Now anger that had been simmering

below the surface pushed itself up. "You know what I'm hearing, Adam?" she asked. "I'm hearing that you don't trust me. I would never ask you questions about parts of your life that are off-limits to me—and I recognize, even if you don't, that everyone has places they don't invite others into. No one's an open book, Adam, so don't pretend that you are."

Adam looked startled by the ferocity of her attack. "Don't turn this around on me, Brandy, I'm warning you . . ."

"You're warning me? Adam, obviously there's a lot you don't know about how human beings work. I don't have time to teach it all to you, though—not if you can't bring yourself to have a little faith in me."

"Brandy . . ." Adam didn't finish the thought. Brandy picked up her purse from the chair where she'd dropped it.

"Think about it. You have my number," she declared. She let herself out and closed the door firmly when she went. Out in the hallway, tears sprang to her eyes. She hadn't meant to storm out—hadn't even meant to spin the whole argument around and make him the bad guy. After all, she *was* keeping secrets.

Secrets of life and death. Secrets she couldn't tell anyone outside the small circle of her summer friends, no matter what.

Dabbing at her eyes with her right hand, she started for the stairs.

Adam sat on his living room sofa, still amazed at what had just transpired. *Did she break up with me?* he wondered. *Because I thought I was breaking up with her.*

Hadn't worked out quite as he expected, though. He had stewed in his suspicions for long enough to work up a good head of moral indignation. Then somehow she had yanked his footing out from under him and made it seem like he was the one with the problem.

Well, I guess I am, he thought. *And my problem is named Brandy Pearson.*

She had been gone less than five minutes when he heard a heavy footfall in the hallway outside his apartment. Brandy? His heart leaped at the thought that she had returned already—confusing, since until he heard the sound he had wanted her out of his life. *Emotions are like that,* he thought. *Can't expect consistency from them.*

He had his hand on the door before she even knocked, and had started to pull it open when a powerful thrust knocked him off his feet.

"Brandy?" he asked, startled. Even furious, she shouldn't be that strong. And when the dark figure swung into the apartment, slamming the door, he knew it wasn't her at all. It was a man—or something like one, anyway. The guy was enormous, the size of a linebacker, and dark, and he looked like he'd fallen into a vat of acid or something. His features were indistinct, as if his face were melting on the spot. And something else—he looked as if he'd been put together from mud and dirty snow, with leaves and branches for skeletal structure. And he stank like the worst locker room Adam had ever been in, multiplied by a thousand.

All this flitted through Adam's mind in less than a second, and he realized that something was terribly wrong. He needed to get out of here, get away from the thing, call for help. Something. But the impossible creature moved quickly, crossing the floor space between the door and where Adam had fallen before Adam could even scramble to his feet. One second he could see the phone, on a side table next to the sofa, not seven feet away. The next, a strong and somehow unclean fist smashed into his face, driving him down again. Intense pain made him screw up his face and shut his eyes. He was pretty sure the thing had broken his nose.

He tried to scramble for the phone again, but he couldn't see through the pain and the tears, and then he felt the creature's hands on him, lifting him into the air and slamming him down again. Miraculously, this time it had chosen to throw him down on the sofa, almost as if it didn't actually want to snap his spine.

Adam forced his eyes to open, just as the thing put its rudimentary face close to his. One of its knees was pressing down on his chest, in real danger, Adam thought, of collapsing his lung. The stench of it was overwhelming, and he nearly gagged. But then the monster spoke in a strangely high and feminine voice, with the most absurd Southern accent.

"Tell me where she is," the voice said. It came from the bizarre man-shaped creature, but Adam could tell it was not *of* him. "Tell me and I won't have to hurt you."

"I—I don't know who you're talking about," Adam managed. "B—Brandy?"

"Season!" the voice answered. Even through the filter of the strange creature, Adam could tell that there was rage behind the response.

"I don't know any Season," he said helplessly.

"Where is she?" the thing demanded again.

"I don't—" The words had barely escaped his lips when the monster swung at him again, its giant fist crashing into his face. It hit him again and again, and he felt blood spray down his shirt, teeth loosen in his mouth, and bones crumble beneath its hammering fists.

6

I've made kind of a point of keeping away from wars, these last many years. Not because I don't love my country, but simply because I have been involved in what amounts to a war of my own, a long, seemingly never-ending campaign against Season Howe. I am both a foot-soldier and an officer in this war, although I grant General status only to Mother Blessing (with whom communication has been sparse of late). And, I suppose, to Season, who is a one-woman army of no small ability.

Kerry held Daniel's journal open on her lap and glanced out the window. Season had said she had an important challenge for her today, and she'd gone to scout conditions. The weather was lovely—clear and crisp, with only a few wispy clouds dotting the blue sky. Kerry didn't know what other conditions might be pertinent, and Season hadn't said.

She liked to read in Daniel's diaries, if only as a way to keep his voice in her head and his life connected to hers. For a while they had been an important learning tool, teaching her things about witchcraft—as well as guiding her to Mother Blessing's home in the Swamp—but now she mostly read them for her own emotional well-being rather than for their educational value.

She turned back to the heavy leather volume and kept reading.

> *But this current conflict, I am sad to say, has become nearly impossible to avoid altogether. It rages across most of the nation, pitting North against South, neighbor against neighbor. As one who takes a somewhat longer view of history than most, I believe there might have been ways to avoid it, but then I am no politician.*

Probably it's best that I am not, for I don't have the temperament for it. Endless discussion and compromise are not my strengths, and though there are certainly politicians who are also decisive men of action, I fear they are few and far between. More of them would rather talk about action than act.

These last few days, however, have been hard for me because I find myself in the middle of it, near a place called Chancellorsville, in my home state of Virginia. I had gone home to the Great Dismal to see Mother Blessing, since my leads on Season had more or less run out, and I hoped that Mother Blessing could find some new way of locating her. There was, of course, military troop movement all around me as I journeyed, but I made myself hard to see and was able to travel unmolested.

I spent two days in my mother's house in the Swamp, enjoying her company and her cooking and being back home for a short while. But then she said she thought that Season had been seen in Washington, so I rode out and headed north.

It didn't take long to realize that there was more troop activity than ever. Confederate forces, the troops of Stonewall Jackson, were manning bulwarks, trying to stand against the advance of Union general Hooker. Hooker, I've heard, hoped to crush the armies of Jackson and Robert E. Lee, but he hesitated too long and Jackson's army surrounded his.

I could see the smoke from miles away, like the entire forest was ablaze. And I could hear the thunder of cannon and later, of rifles. But I had chosen my path and had foolishly decided that keeping to my chosen course was more beneficial than delaying my arrival in Washington by picking a new one. I could weave my way unnoticed through the battle, I was convinced.

I was wrong.

By the time I realized my mistake, I was in the middle of it. The fighting was all around me. The forest was, in fact, on fire. Soldiers ran in every direction, from every direction. Minié balls and bullets flew past. I spoke a few words to Augustus, my horse, to calm him, as the fire and the noise and chaos were driving the poor beast to distraction. I shielded him from the worst of it.

But before I thought to extend the shield to myself, I was hit. A fierce blow knocked me from the saddle, and as I fell to the ground I realized my shoulder had been smashed. I tried to regain my feet, then fell again. Augustus, loyal creature that he is, stayed beside me, but I could not use his strength to help me. Moments later I lost consciousness.

I woke up some time later in a field hospital. A nurse, her uniform torn and bloody, smiled so sweetly that for a moment I thought that she must be a heaven-sent angel. But then she wiped a lock of hair off her face and her hands left a trail of blood across her cheek, and I knew that I yet lived. No angel in heaven ever looked quite so ghastly, I am certain. Confirmation came a moment later, in the form of a jagged-toothed saw she held in the other hand.

"I see you're awake," she said to me.

"I seem to be," I replied. I inhaled,

and the stench of spoiled meat and sewage filled my nostrils. I tried not to show my displeasure. The nurse, it seemed, had become immune to it, just as she seemed to be able to disregard the moans and cries of the injured and infirm that sounded all around us.

"Sorry to see that," she said. "Doc says you've got to lose that arm. Be easier to cut, you were still out."

I glanced at my shoulder, a mangled, repugnant mess of blood and raw meat. I could hardly blame the doctor, who I had not seen as of yet, for wanting to remove as much of it as possible.

Of course, I could have healed it myself given some time and a few herbs and unguents. I probably could have found the appropriate items in the forest myself, if the soldiers had not been in the middle of burning it to the ground.

But now I was in the middle of a field hospital, laid out on a table covered only by a filthy blanket, with, when I turned to look, at least a hundred other wounded soldiers all around me—the source of the shouts of pain, and also of the stink that surrounded me.

If I got up and walked into the woods, surely the nurse would raise some kind of alarm. But if I stayed where I was, she would wield that saw against me. Restoring my shoulder and arm, once they had been butchered, would strain my abilities to the utmost.

If I even survived the surgery. I could see by the pile of bodies stacked up against the wall of a nearby tent that many did not.

"You ready for me to do it?" the nurse asked, indicating with the saw what she meant. "Or do you need a slug of something first?"

I would need several slugs, of some concoction stronger than she might have available, before I would let her near me with that instrument of torture.

"I'm sorry," I told her, "but I have no intention of letting you saw into me with that."

"I don't take it off, gangrene'll set in," she told me. "It'll kill you."

"That's a chance I'll take," I said. I knew that I could mend myself before that happened. But only if I could make my escape from this tool-wielding devil, whom I had once seen as an angel.

"Doctor's orders," she insisted.

I sat up on the rickety table, an action which, to judge from her face, surprised her. She probably hadn't thought I had the strength. "Miss, I do not see a doctor at present. Perhaps if you were to turn your back and attend to some other patient, I would be able to spare you the trouble of either cutting off my limb or further debating with me about it."

She gave me a suspicious glare. "You ain't thinking about killing yourself?"

"Quite the contrary," I assured her. "I'm talking about saving myself."

She looked hurt. "Most of my patients survive," she declared.

Somehow I did not feel comforted. She seemed to be growing more anxious by the minute, and I was worried that she would call out to someone. The more time that went by, the greater the danger that she would be joined by a doctor or another soldier. I decided that it was time to act, if I was going to save myself.

I glanced around quickly, to make sure that we were not yet observed, and then performed a hasty immobilization spell. I was still weak from my wound, and it would not have worked had she been braced against it or expecting it. But for the moment she was stunned into paralysis, simply standing with the wicked saw clutched in her hands and her eyes wide open, watching me.

With her incapacitated, I gingerly climbed off the table, making sure not to upend it. Walking as swiftly as I dared, trying not to attract attention to myself, I made my way through the field of injured, dying, and dead, back toward a corral where I hoped to find Augustus.

I had thought that I was successful in not being seen, but it turned out that I was mistaken. Just as I reached the far edge of the field hospital, a young, hollow-eyed soldier who sat against a tent wall smoking a cigar spoke to me. His left arm was in a bloodied sling, and recent cuts spider-webbed his cheek and jaw. "I seen some-one else do that," he said.

"Do what?" I pretended to be utterly innocent.

"What you done there. Freeze that girl like that."

"I did no such . . . where else did you see that?" A sudden thought changed my sentence midway through.

"Not twenty miles up the road," the young man said. He coughed, a deep, unhealthy, racking cough. "She was like a vision, too. Lot prettier'n you, that's for sure."

"A woman, then?"

"A woman, sure enough." He began to cough again, and this time I wasn't sure he would ever stop. Finally he brought it under control and looked at me with liq-uid eyes. "She stayed at the camp for three days, helping with the wounded. Fixed up many a man I thought would never see another dawn. Finally said she had to move on. But one time, right before she did, one of the boys got a little too friendly *with her. She froze him solid, just like you done."*

"Do you know where she might have gone?"

He laughed, which triggered another coughing fit. "Wish I did," he managed to rasp.

I thanked him and went to look for Augustus. Was it Season he had seen? From his vague description, it could have been. But the Season Howe I was seeking— spending three days helping the wounded in a filthy Army field hospital? More like her, I should think, to wipe them all out with no second thoughts.

Still, if Season it was, then she is not far ahead of me. I put pen to paper in a public house not a day's ride from Washington. If she is still there, perhaps I'll find her in the next day or two.

I remain, Daniel Blessing. Fifth of May, 1863.

It didn't take long for Brandy to realize that she had done Adam a terrible disservice. He had been right, after all. She was hiding things from him. He had every reason not to trust her, and the fact that he didn't was only an accurate assessment of the situation, not a reflection on him.

Three blocks from his place, she stopped short. Probably he'd been leading up to breaking it off with her. She could live with it, if that was the case—she had broken up, and been broken up with, and though she preferred the former neither one would kill her. She was too strong, too independent for that.

So she owed it to him to at least let him have his say, owed him the respect he had earned by being so good to her for so long. If at the end of it he still wanted to call it quits, then fine. She would be okay with it, she was sure.

She turned around and headed back to his apartment. With each step it felt as if a great weight was being lifted off her shoulders. She had felt guilty about walking away, about minimizing his concerns with her own smoke-screen. What she was doing now was a better thing, and she felt good about it.

When she reached the front door to his building she felt a moment's concern. The door was ajar, and she distinctly remembered having shut it when she left. That had been a few minutes before, though, so someone else could have gone out—even Adam himself, she supposed—and left it open.

But worse, there was a muddy print on the door, almost head-high for her. A putrid smell wafted from it. The first thought that entered Brandy's mind almost made her run screaming from the building.

Simulacrum!

There was no guarantee that was it, however, and any number of other possible explanations presented themselves. The melting snows had left the whole city wet and muddy. Anyone could have gotten some gunk on his hands and touched the door. . . .

Still, her heart was pounding as she slipped through the door and into the lobby.

The smell in here was worse, and there were wet footprints on the stairs that led up to Adam's place. Big footprints. Brandy eyed them, swallowing back her terror but ready to run at the slightest provocation.

She already had her cell in her hand as she followed the huge footprints up. Scott's number was still programmed in, so she scrolled to it and held her finger over the SEND button. Walking as quickly as she could while still remaining silent, she hurried down the hall toward Adam's door, stepping beside, instead of on top of, those awful prints.

At Adam's door, the worst was confirmed.

A massive mud print marred its finish. Inside she could hear voices—one of them was Adam's, but it sounded garbled, like he was talking with water in his mouth. She couldn't make out any words, but she knew that it was bad.

She also knew she couldn't handle it alone.

She pressed send.

Scott lived only a few miles from Adam's apartment. He hopped in the RAV4 as soon as he got Brandy's panicked call and drove like a madman the whole way. Ten minutes after his phone had rung, he was screeching to a stop outside the building. Brandy waited outside, terror contorting her face.

He left the car in the street and ran to her, gripping her upper arms anxiously. "Are you okay, Brandy?" he asked.

She nodded and wiped away tears. "I

couldn't stay up there and listen," she said, her voice breaking. She was bordering on hysterical, he thought, as bad as he had ever seen her. "He's hurting Adam."

"There was nothing you could have done about it," Scott assured her. He put his arms around her, and she moved into his hug in a way she hadn't done for a very long time.

"I—I tried to call Kerry," Brandy said, "but I couldn't get through to her. But I reached Rebecca. She promised to keep trying Kerry."

"That's the best thing you could have done. If it is a simulacrum, there's nothing we can do against it."

"Scott, we have to try. Maybe we can just hit it with clubs or something. Anything. It'll kill Adam!"

He hated to ask the obvious, but it needed to be asked. "How do you know it hasn't already?"

"I was up there a couple of minutes ago," she said. "I stood out in the hallway again, just to check. I could still hear Adam's voice, crying for help."

"And there's nobody else in the building?" Scott asked.

"Most everybody works during the day," Brandy said. "There's no super or on-site manager or anything."

Scott nodded. It was just a small building, a family home that had been converted to apartments a decade or two ago. Eight apartments, he guessed, at the most, spread over two stories.

"Okay, then," he said, hoping he sounded much braver than he felt. "Let's go do this."

He led the way into Adam's building, with Brandy clutching his arm so tightly he thought he would lose circulation. Inside, the place stank to high heaven. Heading up the stairs, his courage almost left him—his knees wobbled so much he wasn't sure he could actually make it up unassisted.

Somehow, though, he did. Brandy pointed out Adam's door, as if the giant mud splat on it didn't give it away. Scott thought the whole exercise was kind of silly—there was no way the two of them could do any damage to one of Mother Blessing's manufactured men. But Brandy wanted him to try, so he would. He was no hero, but for him the equation was that simple. Brandy wanted him to try.

In her time of need, she had called him.

Adam's door was closed, but not locked. Scott gulped in a deep breath and hurled it open, afraid of what he would see.

The sight that met him couldn't have been much worse.

Blood was everywhere—more than he thought could possibly come from someone who was still alive. Adam's place was cool and modern, with lots of black steel, glass, and chrome. The glass was spattered with red, the chrome was smeared, and only the black didn't show blood. His off-white Berber carpeting looked like a grisly rainstorm had showered it. Windows looked tinted.

But Adam was still alive. He had rolled into a ball on his sofa, broken and battered. The simulacrum towered over him, no longer beating him but instead simply intimidating the poor man with his unnatural presence. Adam whimpered, and his breathing sounded wet and shallow.

"Get away from him!" Scott demanded. His own throat felt very dry, his muscles tense. If the thing attacked him, he'd end up like Adam or worse. Adam was bigger and stronger than he was. The biggest difference between them was that Scott knew precisely what he was facing. *And somehow,* he thought, *I don't think that's necessarily an advantage.*

Slowly the simulacrum turned, as if gradually becoming aware that there was someone else in the room. It straightened as it regarded Scott and Brandy. Then, as if triggered by the realization of their presence, it charged.

"Scott!" Brandy's voice was little more than an exhalation of breath behind him. Scott trembled, keeping his body between the creature and Brandy. He had been allies with one of these beings once, for a short time. It rode in his car with him. But he had been afraid of it even then. Now he was petrified.

The best he could do was to raise his hands defensively as the creature came toward him. His knees locked, seemingly of their own accord.

Then it was upon him, its surface slick and viscous, its stench overwhelming. Scott opened his hands and clamped them down on the simulacrum's arms, trying to break its charge. The creature barreled into him, knocking him backward a few steps, and Scott felt Brandy's hands on his back, bracing him. Still, the thing's momentum shoved them both back against the wall. Its strength was enormous; Scott knew it could easily tear his head off.

Except it didn't.

Instead, where he held it, the monster began to come undone.

Wet glops of mud and snow fell to Adam's carpeted floor. Bits of tree debris and trash followed. The thing seemed to collapse in on itself and then spill down as if melting under Scott's touch.

"Scott," Brandy said from behind him, only this time her tone was much different than the last time she had spoken his name. Something like awe sounded in her voice. "Scott, what's happening to it?"

He held onto the thing, afraid that if he let go the process would reverse and the monster would re-form. "I don't know," he said. "I guess it doesn't like me."

"I guess it doesn't," Brandy echoed.

The disintegration continued until there was nothing left for Scott to grip. Gunk covered his shoes and left a big pile on the floor, but within moments even that started to dissipate, as if it were evaporating.

"I . . . this is just bizarre," Scott said. "I don't get it."

"I don't either," Brandy said. "But I'm not complaining."

Neither am I, Scott thought. *Neither am I.*

His relief was checked by a sudden anxiety, however. "We'd better check on Adam," he pointed out. "He probably needs a doctor."

Brandy shoved past him to do just that. "We'll need some kind of a story," she said. "We can't tell the paramedics what really attacked him. We'd spend the rest of our lives in a mental hospital. Or prison." She knelt beside Adam and started stroking him gently, comfortingly, speaking so softly that Scott couldn't hear what she was saying. Adam just remained curled in his fetal position, crying quietly.

She was right, Scott knew. They had to come up with a story, and fast. He was already on his way to the phone to dial 911. Help would be here soon, and they'd need to be able to tell them *something.*

The simulacrum was almost completely broken down already, with just a few bits of random detritus remaining on the floor amidst a big muddy stain.

"Okay," Scott said after considering for a few moments. "Here's what we'll say. . . ." Before he had a chance to finish, the emergency operator came on the line, and Scott gave her Adam's address.

By the time he was done, he had almost started breathing normally again. The immediate danger was past.

But one thing was all too certain. Mother Blessing was on their trail again.

Once again Mother Blessing knew the fury of being thwarted by people for whom she had no respect. Those meddling teenagers should have fallen immediately before the might of her creation. Instead, her simulacrum had been defeated by that boy—the one she thought she had been attacking in the first place. She remembered, from her interception of Kerry's communications, that the boyfriend kept better tabs on her location than the girl did. So now that she was ready to continue the battle—to end it—she had waited until she could catch them apart.

But somehow, it had been the wrong boyfriend. He had looked wrong as soon as she saw him through the eyes of her creation. She was committed by then, so she just kept at it, trying to pry from him information that he no doubt truly didn't have. It wasn't until she saw the girl and the boy enter together that she really understood her mistake. The girl was a tramp, or they had broken up.

And even when she realized what had happened, she hadn't known the power that rested in the boy's hands. He was unnatural. He had died, and yet lived—that was the only thing that could explain the simulacrum's response. A creation like that couldn't cohere in the face of the unnatural. A simulacrum's grip on life, Mother Blessing knew, was too tenuous— meeting anything else whose life was false or wrong would cause its immediate dissipation.

So she was angry with them, these children who had defeated her far too often, considering who and what they were. Insignificant insects who muddled along by accident and who needed to be stamped out. They would pay the price, though—once Season was no longer a problem, these others would taste her revenge too, and they would find it painful indeed.

At the same time, she was heartened. Because the girl had made two other calls—one to Kerry, which had not been answered, so Mother Blessing couldn't discern its destination, but the second to Rebecca Levine. Another of their troublesome pack. Rebecca, though, seemed to know where Kerry was. The implication of their conversation was that Kerry was somewhere not too far away—somewhere Rebecca could drive to in a relatively brief time, if need be.

Rebecca was in California. Which meant that she needed to be in California, too. Mother Blessing would not trust a simulacrum to do the whole job this time. So close to Season, she had to be on the scene in person, just in case.

She would leave immediately. This was a war that needed to be finished, and with the Convocation almost upon them, the end had to come soon.

7

Kerry clambered up the side of the cliff as rapidly as she could. Loose dirt and soft stone gave way beneath her hands, but she pressed herself to the wall and dug in with fingers and feet. Jags of rock scraped her cheek. She allowed herself a couple of quick breaths, a moment to collect her thoughts. *What spell can help me here?* she wondered.

None, she decided. This was one of those moments that required physical strength, agility, and courage, not witchcraft. Short of some kind of antigravity spell—or the traditional flying broomstick, which seemed pretty much in the realm of the absurdly mythical—she was on her own.

She glanced up to see how much farther she had to go, and how far out the overhang extended at the top. Heights had never been a particular problem for her, but she decided that there was no advantage to looking down. Nothing but a narrow ribbon of sand, big sharp rocks, and churning surf, thirty feet below her where the ocean carved away the coastline.

Above, Kerry saw some likely handholds, so she stretched for the closest one, shoved the fingers of her right hand into a narrow crevice, and pulled herself up. She raised her right foot to the little shelf on which her right hand had rested a few moments earlier, found firm footing there, and then felt above with her left hand. It was a slow process, but she was no practiced climber.

Almost thirty minutes—and as many scrapes and bruises—later, the overhang was within reach. This would be the tricky part. She'd have to work her way out hand over hand, digging in with her toes, until her back was almost parallel to that narrow beach way down below. The overhang was only four or five feet out, so she wouldn't be in that precarious pose for long, but even a minute or two was distressing. She'd have greatly preferred to scale a section of cliff that was straight at the top—but then, she'd have preferred a hunky instructor and one of those spiffy fluorescent-colored nylon ropes, too. All of which, no doubt, were reasons why Season had picked this spot, which contained none of the above. Kerry had only sneakers, track pants. and a T-shirt on—if she fell, it was going to hurt.

Nothing to be gained by waiting, she decided. She began the excruciating process of holding herself as close as she could to the wall while she inched up and out, feeling gravity trying to yank her back to earth at every moment. Her terror at this stage was almost palpable, and she worried that her palms would sweat so much that she'd lose her grip on the rock face.

A few minutes later, however, she had hold of the upper edge. Some loose dirt and pebbles slid out from under her fingertips, cascading over the cliff and down past her. The clatter when it landed below sounded very far away. Beneath the loose stuff, though, was good solid rock. She pressed her fingers into it so hard she thought she would wear grooves in it.

The last step was to get her left hand up there and haul herself over the top. But her left hand was wedged tightly into a crack in the overhang, and she felt like that was the only thing holding her in place. Her right hand was gripping the upper edge, but if it started to slip, or the edge gave way, there would be nothing to hang on to there.

Stuck, she knew she couldn't make any more progress unless she did something. Gingerly, trying to adhere herself to the face, to glue her feet in position, she worked her left hand free and finger-crawled it up, inch by slow, perilous inch. Finally, she was able to reach the lip with that hand as well.

Now it was a simple matter of letting go with her feet so she could hoist herself up to the top.

Sure. Simple.

But before she got a chance, she heard a movement at the top. A footfall, she thought.

"Season?"

No response.

"Season, is that you?" Kerry demanded urgently.

Still no verbal response. But Kerry gradually became aware of a shadow, a dark form coming over the edge. She hung onto the lip with fingers that trembled from the strain and the anxiety and made herself look up at it.

A tall, sinister man grinned down at her, wearing a long coat that fluttered in the wind at the top of the cliff. His smile looked about as genuine as a ninety-dollar bill.

"Going somewhere?" he asked.

"You want to give me a hand?" Kerry replied, pretty sure she wouldn't accept it if he did. He wasn't one of Mother Blessing's simulacra, she could tell, but that didn't mean he wasn't an ally of some other kind. And she was in about as vulnerable a position as it was possible to find.

"How about a push?" he answered.

Which was all she needed to confirm that he was not exactly a friend. It would be hard to make the right hand gestures while clinging to the edge of the cliff, but she needed to do something to protect herself. So she forced the fingers of her left hand into the appropriate position and spoke one of the ancient words. "*Kalaifa!*"

The man flew from her sight as if swatted away by a giant gust of wind. She knew he had been knocked about twenty feet back, but he was most likely uninjured, unless he'd been speared by a tree branch or something. If he had been just a practical joker, then he'd be fine. If he had more homicidal motives, the immediate threat had been removed and she'd be able to deal with him when she reached the top.

If she hurried. He could still come back and they'd have to do the whole dance all over again. Forcing herself to move faster, she dug in with the fingers of both hands and drew them forward on the top shelf of the cliff, getting some rock and earth under her forearms. The man could already be on his feet, and if he returned all he'd have to do would be to break the grip of one of her hands. Kerry made the decision to finish this now, and kicked free with both feet. She used the momentum to release with her right hand and reach farther out, grabbing ground up to her armpit. Now she could pull her head up over the top. The man was still in the dirt where she had thrown him, glaring at her. She tossed him a quick smile and began hoisting herself up.

A moment later she was safely on the top of the cliff, standing up and dusting herself off.

The man turned indistinct, as if she were looking at him through a wall of Jell-O, and then took on solid form again. This time the form was that of Season Howe, who rubbed her bottom as she smiled at Kerry.

"Ow," she said. "Good job, Kerry."

"Thanks." Kerry touched one of the raw spots on her cheek. "Now maybe you can tell me what that was all about."

"A test," Season said simply. "In the time we have left before the Convocation, there's not a whole lot I can still teach you. But I can test what you've learned, and make sure your reactions are appropriate. So far, so good."

Kerry Profitt's diary, March 12.

The ways in which this whole business is like school are numerous. I have always loved reading and writing, but the reading program Season has put me on is almost ridiculous—especially since so many of her magic texts were written back in practically prehistoric times, so the language is all stiff and ancient. Thanks to Season's magic translator (just like with the books Mother Blessing showed me, way back when), I can read the books that look like Latin or Greek or German or whatever. At first glance they're in a foreign language, but when I look at them again, I can make out the words just as if they were written in English. Sometimes bad English, but English just the same. Fortunately I have Daniel's journals, and a few books the Morgans have left around the house, to give me a break.

And then the testing part! Like earlier today, when I had to scale this giant freaking cliff while she stood at the top, casting a glamour to make herself look like some kind of scary bad guy. I never had a midterm like that in high school. Would have reduced class size a bit if we had, I guess. Don't let the PTA know.

I get the idea behind it, of course. We don't know exactly what we're going to be facing, either in more possible battles with Mother Blessing or at the Witches' Convocation. Chances are I won't be forced to climb any cliffs. But I might be put into situations where physical strength and/or bravery are required. So better to know now that I can do it, right? If I had fallen today, ouch. Broken leg, whatever. Or maybe Season had some kind of plan to magically break my fall, although of course she wouldn't have told me that. But if I didn't learn my limits, and then wimped out while facing one of MB's bad things, it could be serious trouble for me and for Season.

So, the testing. And in between, the reading. And in between all of that, the purification rites. Also important, Season says. Not that I've been around any guys with whom to be impure, but she says it's not just that. It's the atmosphere, which is chock-full of pollution and nasty microbes and stuff. It's the gunk we pick up from flies and doorknobs and those buttons you press on the hot air hand dryer in the ladies' room, and also that whole breathing thing. In other words, not just purity of spirit but also of body. Helps make the magic work better, somehow. The impurities in a witch's system act like little blocking agents, she says, impeding the flow of the forces that we channel through ourselves. Like shopping carts and old cars tossed into a riverbed. Take out all the crap and everything moves more smoothly down the correct channels.

The purification rituals take many forms. My favorite is the long, hot baths with lilac petals floating in the tub. Not so great is the standing with arms outstretched and a ten-pound weight in each hand for thirty minutes, while counting backward from a thousand. Season swears both kinds are necessary, along with several others. At least she does them with me (although with the bath one, we go one at a time). By the time we go to the Convocation we will be two pure chicks, I gotta say. And looking just fine in our plain white robes, which is what we wear for this drill.

More later.

K.

By the time they left Adam at Mass General, he had been admitted and sedated. He had tried to give the paramedics and the police his version of events, but Brandy and Scott had been there to intercede with their own translation of his garbled tale.

They had agreed to stick as close to the literal truth as possible. The way they told it, Adam and Brandy had had a fight, and Brandy walked out. But she had second thoughts and went back. By the time she got back, someone had broken into the apartment. Brandy could hear a struggle or heated argument through the door but was afraid to go in, so she called Scott. He came over, and by the time they went inside the assailant had fled. They found Adam, beaten and hysterically raving about a monster—no doubt a really big burglar—and called 911. No, neither of them had seen the assailant—he must have run away while Brandy was waiting outside for Scott. No, she couldn't think of any enemies Adam might have, and she couldn't identify anything that was missing. But she had only known him for a few months, and there might, of course, have been something in his past that she didn't know about.

The police and medical personnel seemed to buy the story. She and Scott told it essentially the same way when they were questioned separately and together, and anyway, it all made so much more sense than Adam's ravings. The fact that Adam's were true didn't enter into it—it was the appearance of truth they were after, not the real thing. Anyway, Brandy reasoned, they weren't under oath, so it wasn't like they were committing perjury.

Lying, yes. But with good cause.

When they were allowed to leave, they sat in Scott's car out in the hospital parking lot, giving themselves some decompression time before he took her home. Brandy looked over at Scott, illuminated by light that washed in from one of the hospital's street lamps. He looked different than he had before, even at Christmas, somehow—strong, capable, decisive. There was a set to his jaw, a sense of determination expressed by a slight stiffening of his lips, a resolve signaled by a narrowing of his eyes, that she had never seen before.

She liked what she saw.

"You were pretty amazing, Scott," she said quietly.

"What? I had no idea that thing would fall apart. I still wish I knew why."

"I don't mean just that," Brandy said. She didn't want him to think it had been an empty compliment, or worse, a backhanded one. Because that kind of thing had never been beyond her. But it wasn't her intention now. "I mean, that was cool too. But the whole thing. Answering when I called, riding to the rescue like that. A lot of guys wouldn't do that if their ex called up and said her new boyfriend was in trouble."

"What, I'm supposed to just shrug and say, 'whatever'?" Scott answered. "He means a lot to you. You mean a lot to me. That's just the way it is."

"That's exactly what I mean," Brandy said.

"You don't even think it's special. You just did it, because that's what a person does. In your world, at least."

Scott shrugged, as if he didn't even get what a big deal it was.

Which was when Brandy realized that the warm spot she held for him in her heart had never completely gone away. Sure, it had cooled. Right down to a frosty chill, for a while. But the embers had still been glowing, she just hadn't seen them. Now, though, she felt as if they were being fanned, fresh air being blown in by one of those big old-fashioned bellows. Heat radiated from her core.

She leaned toward him, touching his arm. "Scott, I—"

"Listen, Brandy," he interrupted, completely oblivious. He stared straight out the windshield as he spoke, not even looking at her. "You'll probably kick me or something for saying this, but it's something I have to get off my chest. I was an idiot."

"You were?"

"Absolutely," Scott insisted. "I mean, I was kind of obsessed with Kerry. You knew that— you probably knew it before I did. But that was just stupid, that grass is always greener stuff. Kerry's an amazing person, sure. But so are you. You're beautiful, and you're the most insightful, perceptive person I've ever known, and you were right in front of me the whole time. Right in my own apartment, my own bed. So getting all hung up on Kerry like that, and spoiling what we had . . . well, I was a dope. I'm sorry. If there was any way I could undo it, I would."

Brandy could hardly believe what she was hearing. Especially since it was so close to what she was feeling right now. She recognized that it might simply have been a reaction to their mutual brush with death, which often drew people together in an artificial intimacy.

But she didn't think so. Instead, she thought the experience had knocked blinders away from their eyes that they had consciously placed there, not realizing what a mistake it had been.

She placed a hand on his leg and squeezed gently. "I think maybe we can work on it."

His face brightened instantly, and he finally met her gaze. "Do you mean it?"

"Sure," she said without hesitation. "If

people can decide to break up, they can certainly decide to un-break up, right?"

"Isn't that usually called making up?"

"Yes," Brandy admitted. "But that sounded too much like a golden oldie. Then again, there's always making out. Which maybe we could talk about too."

"Talking about it seems so . . . I don't know. Counterproductive."

She snuggled a little closer to him. "Well, I guess we don't have to do that much talking."

He started to lean toward her, then suddenly sat upright. "Oh, crap!"

"What?" she asked, startled. She turned in her seat, to see if he had noticed something out her window. *Another attacker?*

"I just remembered, in all the craziness with Adam and everything, we never called Rebecca to tell her we're okay. We should do that, and make sure she lets Kerry know what's happened."

Brandy realized her heart was racing and adrenaline pumping from his sudden motion. "Okay," she said. "Let's give her a call." Rebecca, being Rebecca, would almost certainly be freaking out by now, Brandy knew.

She dug her cell from her purse and flipped it open abruptly—glad that Scott had remembered, but upset because she would rather that his attention had been solely focused on her at that moment.

Just the way he is, I guess, she thought. *If I'm going to be with him—and it looks like maybe I am, strange as that seems—I've just got to be able to live with it.* She knew she would have to visit Adam in the hospital. There would be awkward questions. But then, life refused to be as orderly as she wanted.

She dialed Rebecca, and a moment later their friend, breathless and anxious, came on the line.

8

Exactly what she feared had happened. It was all starting up again, and this time a complete noncombatant, the proverbial innocent bystander, had been injured. And Mother Blessing was still after them—this proved it, without a doubt.

Rebecca couldn't reach Kerry and Season on the phone. She rushed about the house, in a near panic. She had to go up to Bolinas, had to find them and let them know what was happening. It would only be a few hours by car. She wanted to wait for Erin to get home from a late class, but as the minutes ticked by she began to worry that Erin wouldn't be coming home—that she was studying late in the library, or had a date, or something. She paced, she tried to sit and gather her thoughts, but then she squirmed and jumped to her feet again. *Come home, come home, come home,* she silently pleaded. But Erin didn't, and the girl refused to carry a cell phone or pager to class. Something about respecting the lecturer, which Rebecca kind of understood. But then, Erin had never been attacked by a witch.

Since it didn't look like she would show up any time soon, Rebecca settled for leaving her housemate a note. That was probably better anyway, she decided upon reflection, because with a note, Erin couldn't ask any nosy questions. She scrawled, "Erin, I'm out of town for a day or so. I'll call you when I can. Love, Beck," on a sheet of ripped-out notebook paper and pinned it to the kitchen table with a salt shaker.

She didn't, in fact, know if she would even spend a single night away, or if she'd be driving back here much later that night. But if she found Season and Kerry tonight, there was every likelihood that they would insist she stay over. It would be very late by the time she reached the Morgan house. And if she didn't find them at first, she wouldn't be back here until she did, however long that might take.

She tossed some clean underwear, a blouse, and a skirt into her backpack, then put in a toothbrush and toothpaste and a hairbrush. Certain there were things she was forgetting, she decided that nothing else was that important anyway. Outside, a hard, steady rain had been pounding Santa Cruz all evening. Her old VW was parked across the street, and she had almost reached it when she remembered her wallet and cell phone, inside on top of her dresser. She ran back in, fetched those items, stuffed them into the backpack with everything else.

Back in the rain, she dashed toward the car, already wet from her first aborted attempt.

Before she reached it, however, an abrupt movement caught her eye. A dark shape separated from the background, and Rebecca realized it was someone coming toward her. She broke into an all-out sprint, but the shape was much too fast for her. By the time she tried to jam her key into the car's door lock, he was on her.

The man slammed into her, hard, and one of his hands grabbed her wrist, yanking it away from the car door. Only a faint glow filtered from the streetlights through the heavy rain, but that, and the smell, were enough to tell Rebecca that she didn't face a man at all, but one of Mother Blessing's awful simulacra.

She twisted out of its grasp, maybe helped by the rain—its hands seemed slick, and she slid from between them as if she'd been oiled—but she only made it a couple of staggered steps before she tripped over her own feet. The thing came at her again, swatting her as she tried to rise and knocking her sprawling in the wet street. Her face skidded on the pavement, her fingers clutching at it as she tried desperately to right herself. So far the thing had made no sound, and she knew that she should scream but couldn't seem to find her breath.

Instead, she pushed herself to her knees again, and then to her feet, and then it had her, one powerful arm wrapped about her middle. She finally was able to let out a scream, but the creature clamped its other hand over her mouth. Rebecca struggled against it, kicking and squirming, all to no avail. It was far stronger than she was, and she couldn't hurt it. After a moment it moved its hand up to cover her nose as well as her mouth. She gulped for breath but couldn't find it, and seconds after that, the darkness of the night had engulfed her completely.

"A lot of people think witches are inherently evil," Season said. She and Kerry sat in the cramped living room, listening to the wind whistle in the eaves. "That we're in league with the devil. That we're always having unnatural relations with goats. In fact, if there's a devil, I've never met him, and while I enjoy feta cheese on Greek salads, that's the closest I've been to a goat in at least a hundred years."

Kerry laughed at that. It was late and she was in sweats and fuzzy socks, ready for bed. She had been on her way there when Season called her into the living room, apparently in a reflective mood.

"That's why witches have been persecuted so much?" Kerry asked. She had become used to Season's enforcement of the fifteen-questions routine, and it didn't apply after "school hours" were over. "Because of the goats?"

"One of the reasons," Season acknowledged with a nod. "People often tend to fear what they don't understand. Since our abilities are beyond the scope of most people, beyond what they can possibly ever experience for themselves, they decide that there must be something sinister behind us.

"Of course, witches like Mother Blessing don't help matters any. Whenever people have unreasonable fears and prejudices, if they can point to a specific individual who seems to embody that prejudice, then it's that much easier for them to lump all the rest of that group in the same category. Mother Blessing and the few other witches around who are genuinely evil make good poster children for those who hate witches."

"What if witches made themselves known to the world at large?" Kerry wondered. "If you weren't all hiding all the time, if witches were common knowledge, maybe they'd be accepted better?"

Season hesitated for a moment before answering, looking deep into Kerry's eyes as she did. "How often has that proven not to be true?" she said finally. "Think about African Americans, who were enslaved for hundreds of years, and in some cases are still having a hard time being admitted into parts of American society, a hundred and some years after emancipation. As a group, they still don't have income equity with whites. Think about gay people—we've known about them forever, and look at their struggles with acceptance. I'm not saying that witches are a persecuted minority, exactly. We are, but in a very different way. There are so few of us we'll never have a big voting bloc or anything like that, even if there were issues on which we would want to vote in lockstep. But we aren't lacking for power. It's not political, necessarily, but we have other forms of power."

"Okay, point taken," Kerry admitted. "Maybe coming out as witches isn't the best idea."

"It's never been anything but trouble in the past," Season agreed. "A lot of us still have bad memories of the Inquisition, and Salem, that kind of thing. We seem to be better off staying in the shadows. The whole low profile bit."

"I guess it's a good thing I have the voice of experience here to guide me," Kerry said, "so I don't shoot my mouth off at the Convocation and say something stupid."

"You're lucky you're so young for your first Convocation," Season pointed out. "By the time you go to your second, you'll be the one with all the experience."

That'll be five hundred years, Kerry thought, blown over by the hugeness of that concept. *Will I even still be alive then?* "That's a pretty big commitment," she said.

Season cocked her head to the right and showed her a surprised face. "I thought you were ready to make it."

Kerry didn't quite know what to say. "I . . . I thought I was too. I mean, I think I am. But . . . you know, I'm young. What if I decide I'd rather be a firefighter or a dentist or something?"

"You're joking."

"About those two particular career choices, yes. Not that there's anything wrong with them. But you know what I mean. I'm eighteen. How many eighteen-year-olds do you know who figure out what they want to do with the rest of their lives at that age and then stick to it? Most people I've known haven't even stuck to a single college major, much less a career. Much less a career that could last well beyond the usual forty years or so."

Season let out a small sigh. "I know it's asking a lot, Kerry," she said. "Witches live a very long time. It's a serious commitment. Believe me, there have been times that I've regretted the decision too. But not many, and they always pass."

"Well, you're kind of stuck, right? I mean, once you pass a hundred and twenty or so, it must be kind of hard to suddenly decide you didn't mean to be a witch after all."

"It happens," Season admitted. "Just not very often, and the consequences aren't pretty."

"I bet not," Kerry agreed. She tried unsuccessfully to stifle a huge yawn. "I'm totally beat," she said. "I guess I'll see you in the morning."

"Another big day," Season promised. "Almost time to leave for the Convocation."

Another yawn escaped Kerry. "I can't wait."

When Rebecca woke up, she felt sick and sore all over. It took her a minute to realize that some of the soreness was because she hadn't been able to move her arms or legs for what must have been hours—she was tied to a stiff wooden chair in what looked like a long-abandoned kitchen.

Light streamed in through warped sheets of plywood nailed over a window, illuminating a stained and faded linoleum floor and gutted cabinets, the sink and appliances long since taken away. There were two other chairs in the room with her, and a wall calendar from 1996, but nothing else except dust, cobwebs, and a black growth on one wall that must have been mold.

Light, she realized. She had been here all night, then. As she tried to turn in the chair to see what was behind her, a wave of nausea passed through her. Her head throbbed, as if someone had been using it to drive nails through concrete.

She remembered the night before—being grabbed on her way to the car. One of Mother Blessing's artificial goons. She couldn't recall anything at all after that, so he must have knocked her out, then brought her—where? Wherever this was, some old empty house. Hours had passed, though, so she could be just about anywhere. Maybe not even in Santa Cruz anymore. She couldn't smell the ocean, but the house's close, musty air overwhelmed any odors that might have leaked in from outside.

The house had a hollow feel, as if it had been vacant for a long time. She was pretty sure she was completely alone. If the thing that had brought her here—or anyone else—was here now, she couldn't see him. She couldn't see much, though. She could try to jerk the whole chair around, but at the moment such a violent motion would probably only succeed in making her vomit or pass out again. *Anyway,* she thought, *the old witch makes those things out of found materials, right? So he could just be a bunch of spiderwebs and mold right now, but ready to pop up as soon as I make a move.*

The most pressing question was the hardest to answer. Why? What good did it do Mother Blessing to have Rebecca locked away in a house? There had been the attack on Brandy's boyfriend, too—was there some new battle going on that they were all going to be sucked into? Had things heated up to this point?

Well, duh, she thought. *I wouldn't be tied to a chair if* something *wasn't going on.*

Through the nausea, she realized two urgent things. She was very hungry, and she really, really had to pee.

Somehow, it didn't look like either need would be satisfied very soon.

From somewhere behind her—somewhere else in the house—a door opened, groaning on its hinges, then closed with a loud bang. Rebecca started, as if the bang had been immediately behind her head. She suddenly felt terribly vulnerable. She was completely immobilized, unable even to turn around to face whoever had entered the house. She could hear floorboards squeaking as if under a ponderous weight. Slowly, the squeaking came nearer.

Rebecca's eyes were wide with fright. Who was it? The simulacrum that had brought her here? Someone else—even a random stranger? Maybe it was someone who could rescue her. That was a pleasant thought, but probably too good to be true. It was far more likely to be someone with a nefarious motive. A few minutes before she had been wishing that there was someone else with her, but now she realized that alone was far safer than trapped here with the wrong kind of company.

"Who's there?" she demanded, trying to sound belligerent, as if she had any control whatsoever over the situation. "Speak up!"

"Now, don't y'all worry 'bout me," a feminine voice said. The Southern accent was so thick it almost sounded cartoonish to Rebecca's ears, accustomed as she was to the way New Yorkers and Californians spoke. "I'm just here to have a little talk, aren't I?"

"How would I know?" Rebecca replied. "Why don't you untie me so we can have a real conversation?"

A soft chuckle. "Well, now, I don't think that'd be very smart, do you? Not very smart at all, Miss Levine. Or can I call y'all Rebecca?"

"Untie me, and you can call me anything you want," Rebecca shot back. The speaker still hadn't shown herself, but Rebecca knew who it was. Who it had to be. Mother Blessing. Daniel's mother. Kerry had described her way of speaking, even imitated her a couple of times. And, of course, Rebecca herself had heard the voice before, only filtered through the voicebox of an inhuman being, one of the witch's simulacra. "Are you going to let me see you, Mother Blessing?"

Another laugh met this question. "Well, ain't you just the cleverest little thing?" More moaning floorboards. Rebecca could hear the huffs of the woman's breath as she walked, seemingly with effort, across the kitchen. A moment later, a vast field of powder blue polyester hove into view. Mother Blessing was enormous, one of the biggest women Rebecca had ever seen. If her thighs, wrapped in that tight polyester, were tree trunks, her waist was one of those redwoods that they cut tunnels through to let cars drive under. She smiled a ghastly grin at Rebecca, the pancake creasing and cracking on her face, the foothills of blue eye shadow leading toward mountains of platinum hair piled on her head in one of the world's biggest beehives.

"No mirror where you live?" Rebecca asked defiantly.

One of Mother Blessing's meaty hands slapped her across the face. *The woman can move fast when she wants to,* Rebecca realized. She had barely seen the slap coming. Even if she had, she wouldn't have been able to dodge it.

"I'm sure y'all are smarter than that," Mother Blessing said. There was no humor in her voice anymore, nothing but anger and an edge of bitterness. "I'm sure y'all don't want to make this any harder on either of us than it has to be."

"That all depends," Rebecca said, her insolent attitude only heightened by the slap. "Just what is 'this' going to be?"

"Just a short little conversation," Mother Blessing assured her. "Y'all are going to tell me where to find Season and Kerry, and then I'll untie you and leave you alone. Now that sounds fair, doesn't it?"

"Yeah, fair," Rebecca said. "Only, I don't think so. In fact, I think you ought to take yourself a flying—"

Again, Mother Blessing moved faster than Rebecca could have imagined. This time, the slap spun her head around to one side, and she saw flashes of bright light when it connected.

Note to self, Rebecca thought. *No profanities around this freak.*

9

Scott was almost frantic.

Hours had passed since they had called Rebecca to warn her about the attack on Adam, and what that might portend for the rest of them. Rebecca had promised to get in touch with Kerry and let her know about it. Kerry and Season were the only ones who would know what to do, how to respond.

If at all. If there was any reasonable response possible.

But Rebecca had not called back. He and Brandy had taken turns trying her, at home and on her cell, through the night. Neither had slept much. Rebecca's roommate Erin had finally unplugged her phone, apparently, after answering with less and less good humor, then finally insisting that they stop calling. But they hadn't. And they wouldn't, until they talked to Rebecca, or Kerry.

Now the sun had risen, shining down onto New England. It would still be dark in California, Scott knew, but not for long. Daylight would race across the continent, illuminating forests and villages, cities and plains, mountains and rivers, and finally the far coast.

The coast where Rebecca was in some kind of trouble—where Mother Blessing was closing in on them. Scott was certain of it.

"We need to catch a plane," he announced when Brandy came into the room. Her hair was a mess, her eyes puffy and bloodshot from lack of sleep, and she sipped from a Red Bull. They were at her apartment, where they had spent the night. She had tried to grab a few winks from time to time, unsuccessfully. Scott had alternated between pacing, dialing the phone, and staring out the window at the dark city. Once he had taken a shower, just to try to clear the cobwebs from his mind, but then he'd had to put back on the same clothes, reeking with sweat from the fight and everything since. The mood that had come over them before, the definite rekindling of heat between them, hadn't gone away, but it had been overshadowed by other events.

"Do we have a reservation?" Brandy asked, confused.

"No," he said. "So I guess we're paying full fare. Don't worry, I'll take care of it. But we have to get to California. San Jose is closest, I guess, to Santa Cruz. I wish we knew where Kerry and Season were so we could go straight there, but we need to check in on Rebecca anyway."

"Don't you think that might be a little extreme, Scott?" Brandy wondered. "A cross-country flight because she's been away from her phone for a few hours?"

"Was what that thing did to Adam extreme?"

Brandy nodded, catching on. "I'll get my purse."

Rebecca tried to think about anything except the pain.

Her friends had often called her a retro hippie, and she figured that was why she fit in so well at UC Santa Cruz—even in the twenty-first century, it was the biggest hippie school in the state.

Part of what made her a hippie, she guessed, was her preference for nonviolence, for passive resistance to injustice. It had been the most effective technique for those protesting the Vietnam war or fighting for civil rights in the sixties. Don't fight back, show that you are above violence by refusing to sink to that level. Demonstrate that there's a better way.

She tried to cling to that belief, but it was hard. Her flesh had been burned by at least fifty matches. She'd been pinched, pulled, slapped, punched hard in the abdomen. Her hair had been pulled, twisted, and yanked. If Mother Blessing had had a pair of pliers Rebecca was sure her fingernails would be gone by now, and probably only the lack of plumbing in the house had kept the old water torture thing from happening.

But she had refused to tell the witch anything. Friendship was more important than physical discomfort, and violence was an insult that could be dealt with only by absolute rejection. Telling Mother Blessing where Kerry was would be disastrous, and Rebecca would withstand any torture rather than reveal her location.

At least she would try.

Kerry was her friend, someone for whom Rebecca would do anything she could. Anything on Earth.

She had stopped trying to reason with the woman. Mother Blessing wanted what she wanted, and there was no getting past that barrier. She had said she wanted to talk, but that wasn't true. She only wanted to listen, and then just to the specific answer that she sought.

Rebecca had tried, early on, to persuade Mother Blessing of the hopelessness of her effort. "Do you know what my last name is?" she had asked, ignoring the fact that the old witch had used it when she first came into the kitchen. "It's Levine. That's my dad's name. My mother was a Yelinsky. Her grandparents lived in Poland in the 1930s. They were Jewish. You know what that means, right? You were around in those days. Of course, you were probably on the other side."

Mother Blessing hadn't responded—verbally, at least. Instead she had struck another match and held the flame in front of Rebecca's eyes. Rebecca had blown it out, and Mother Blessing had quickly jammed the still-burning head into the soft skin right beneath Rebecca's left eye.

Rebecca screamed, and tears that she thought had dried up started to fall again. "It means they were in a concentration camp," Rebecca said when she could compose herself enough to speak. "They lived through worse torture than you could even imagine with your pitifully small mind. And I'm here, which means they survived it. They survived all that horror, so there is nothing you can do to me—"

Another match struck. "You can make this stop," Mother Blessing whispered, repeating the same chorus she had been singing for a while now. "You can put an end to the whole thing. It's easy. Just tell me what I want to know."

"—nothing you can do to me that is worse than what they went through. There is no way you can make me tell you anything, so just give it up. If you do, I won't tell Season what you've done, and she won't kick your butt for it."

Stories of her family's history had meant nothing to Mother Blessing, so Rebecca stopped speaking them out loud. But they meant a great deal to her. Her great-grandparents were many years gone now, but she had met them as a young girl. She had seen the numbers tattooed on their wrists, had heard the tales they told to adult friends when they thought young Rebecca was sound asleep in her bed. She filled her mind with those tales, the unspeakable things her great-grandparents had seen, had lived through, and with thoughts of Kerry, good, brave Kerry, and she bit the insides of her cheeks until she tasted blood, and she withstood the pain.

She had to.

She *couldn't* give up, *couldn't* turn over Kerry and Season to the old witch. Mother Blessing was a coward who preferred to let others do her dirty work for her. Rebecca didn't know much about her, but she knew that. The fact that she was here, that she was getting her own hands dirty, meant that things were coming to a head. Some kind of endgame was in the works.

Well, Rebecca would be happy to see it all end. But on Kerry's schedule, and Season's. On their terms. Not Mother Blessing's.

She had never thought of herself as a particularly courageous person, though she had been moved and touched when Kerry had told her that she was. She still didn't think so. *Stubborn, yes. Intransigent. Not brave.*

She didn't even think she was brave when she finally lost consciousness.

The girl would *not* give up.

Mother Blessing had thought she was the softest of the bunch, the weakest link, as it were. A couple of hard tugs on her shiny red hair and the girl would rat out her friends just to make it stop.

She was surprised, and, she had to admit, somewhat impressed, by the girl's fortitude. Annoyed, too. It just made her work harder than she had hoped to. Sweat filmed her forehead and upper lip, and she was dying for some sweet tea and a Hershey bar. There was none of that in this house, however. It was an abandoned place on the edge of town, this awful Santa Cruz place, with plywood over the windows and a CONDEMNED sign tacked to the front door. Mother Blessing couldn't wait to get out of the house, out of Santa Cruz. If she never had to come back to California again it would be too soon. Her son had died in California, after all. And met Kerry in California.

In some ways, this was where it had all started, this recent cycle of violence and war that led toward the Convocation. *Fitting that it should end here,* she thought.

The girl had lapsed into unconsciousness now, though. Mother Blessing hadn't expected to have to expend this kind of effort on her, but since she had, she was angry with the girl, and therefore less inclined than she might otherwise have been to spare her any unnecessary discomfort.

So since the girl wouldn't talk, she would extract the information she wanted in a different way. A little easier for her, a lot harder on the girl. Mother Blessing offered a halfhearted shrug. Didn't really matter to her, one way or the other.

She looked at Rebecca Levine, her head slumped forward onto her chest, mouth slack, body finally relaxed against the cords that held her in the chair. She was a pretty girl who could have grown into a beautiful woman. Not now, though. Pity she had brought this on herself. Mother Blessing put her right hand on

Rebecca's head, feeling the girl's soft hair and the tight, unyielding flesh underneath, close against her skull. She applied more pressure, and at the same time spoke a single word in the ancient language of magic.

Her fingertips dug through the flesh, as if it were no more dense than the thick mud of her home swamp. Pressing harder, they bit into the skull, crumbling bone like stale bread. Beneath the skull there was brain matter, softer still and a little wet beneath her probing hand.

Mother Blessing closed her eyes and concentrated as her fingers rooted around in Rebecca's brain. The girl's thoughts flew into her mind scattershot, as if someone were drumming on the remote control of a TV with a thousand channels. Worries about school and work and Mother Blessing herself, fears, joys, loves, and hates. The simple pleasure of sand between her toes at the beach, and the more recent horror of being attacked in the dark and awakening, bound, all alone in a strange place. A recipe for chocolate chip cookies. A memory of a winter morning in Central Park with her father, trying to ice skate for the first time. An image of a pelican skimming across the waves, its wingtips dipping into the water.

And finally, a name—Morgan—and a town.

Bolinas.

That's where Kerry and Season were.

Mother Blessing pulled her hand out of Rebecca's skull and shook her fingers as if she had just touched raw sewage.

"There, now, that wasn't so bad, was it?" she asked the lifeless girl.

Rebecca, of course, didn't respond.

That was okay. She had what she needed. She would leave Rebecca's body here. Somebody would find it, one of these days, but probably not soon. Not in this abandoned place. And Mother Blessing would never be connected to it, at any rate.

Anyway, she needed to get to Bolinas, wherever that was. She had a map of California that she'd bought at the airport out in her stolen car.

No simulacra this time. They had helped with Rebecca, to a point. But they wouldn't stand up against Season and Kerry. That had been proven. Still, she needed to keep them pinned down until she could get there herself, needed to make sure they didn't run away yet again.

She had an idea, though. One that would do the job just fine.

She could almost taste victory now, and it was sweet.

10

A steady spring rain had tapped against walls and windows all evening. Kerry was amazed that there had been so much rain in northern California over the winter and in the days leading up toward the Convocation. Season assured her that everything she thought she knew about weather was changing, faster than she could probably imagine.

"Call it global warming, global climate change, whatever you want," Season said. "It's happening. Most people don't live long enough to see the progression firsthand, but I have. Up in the Sierra Nevada mountains, not so far from here, glaciers are receding, and winter's snows melt much sooner than they used to. The Antarctic ice shelf is thinning and weakening. Ocean currents are changing. It's getting worse, and it's happening in a hurry. The snap of a finger in geologic time. It's already reaching the point that people who haven't lived as long as me can observe some of the changes, if they're paying attention."

"Can't you—or we, you know, witches, can't we do something about it?" Kerry asked anxiously.

"You think we aren't?" Season responded. "You should see what things would be like if we weren't butting in as much as we're able. We have a group constantly trying to help mitigate the damage that humans do to one another and to their planet, but there's only so much they can accomplish. As a people, we seem able to create war, famine, environmental catastrophe, and crime no matter what. Against that, witches can only try to hold the line. I told you that we're engaged in a continual struggle between chaos and order. The human tendency supports the chaos side, so it's an uphill climb. But we're still trying, all the time."

Kerry was about to respond when a loud crack sounded outside, and virtually simultaneously the living room window shattered, glass crashing to the floor in great shards. A hot buzz swept through the room and thudded into the far wall, between the two women. Kerry jumped, her heart slamming into her throat. "What—?"

"Get down!" Season commanded. She dove across the space separating them and pushed Kerry to the floor. They both landed hard against the threadbare rug. "Someone's shooting at us," Season explained.

Kerry hadn't known what to expect, but somehow that was worse than anything she would have thought of. She was accustomed to magical attacks, or as close to accustomed to them as she figured one could be. But a bullet . . . that was so brutal, so cold. Witchcraft, magic—these things were part of nature, inextricably tied to it. A few ounces of lead formed into a killing instrument was decidedly unnatural and filled Kerry with revulsion.

"Who . . . ?" she began. She didn't bother to finish. *Who else?* Somehow Mother Blessing had found them.

She didn't usually use bullets, though. She had seen for herself how useless they were against Season.

Against Season . . . but not against Kerry. Had that shot been meant just for her? Take out Season's ally, and then go up against Season one-on-one? Kerry shivered, and not just from the cold air that streamed in through the broken window.

"We should find out who," Season suggested. Staying low, she crawled to the wall beneath the large window. She motioned to Kerry to keep down, even as she lifted her own head to the windowsill and peered out.

"Who's out there?" Kerry inquired urgently. Her terror was quickly moving toward rage. She felt violated by the attack and wanted to take some kind of action.

"It's—down!" Season dropped her own head below the edge of the window again, just as another bullet whipped through some of the remaining glass. Shards showered onto her head.

"There are a few of them," Season told her.

"But who are they?"

"I don't know," Season answered. "They just look like regular guys. Like hunters, I guess. A couple in camouflage clothing, others in normal street clothes. They're all carrying guns, and they're spreading out—it looks like they're trying to surround the house."

"But . . . they can't do that! Why?"

"I have to think Mother Blessing is behind it somehow," Season replied.

"I got that much."

"Then you know as much as me," Season snapped. "Sorry," she said a second later. "I'm just trying to figure this out. It's a new tactic, but it's still part of the same war, I'm sure."

Kerry was quiet for a moment, listening hard. Outside she could hear soft voices and the occasional snap of a twig or rustle of leaves, but for the most part the movements of their hunters were masked by the patter of the rain, which now blew inside through the shattered window. They could have been closing on the house, for all she could tell—about to burst in at any moment.

"She's controlling them," Season ventured. "I don't know where she found them, maybe just around the community. They don't look like men who know they're engaged in a life-or-death task—their faces are kind of blank, so I'm sure she's taken them over. But still, they won't be as easy to deal with as simulacra."

"Why not?" Kerry wondered out loud. "They're just humans, right? And if they're not altogether there, they should be—"

"That's exactly why," Season explained. "Their humanity. They can think, they can reason, and they can communicate. Mother Blessing may be behind them, controlling them, but she left them enough of their own personalities to allow them to become an effective unit."

"Great," Kerry said. "Then what do we do?" A horrible thought struck her. "Do we have to kill them?"

"I'm thinking," Season said, her tone bordering on impatience again. "If they were simulacra, I wouldn't hesitate to blast them. But they're human—we can't just kill them. Not only would it be wrong, but it would negate all the purification rituals we've just put ourselves through. We'd have to start over, and there's no way we'd be ready for the Convocation."

Another sound from outside, a footstep on gravel. The men were closer now. Neither Season nor Kerry had shown themselves at the window, so no more shots had been fired, but Kerry was convinced that wouldn't last long.

As soon as the men were inside, she and Season would be the proverbial sitting ducks.

"Can we disable them in some way?" Kerry asked. "Immobilize them, paralyze them, something?"

"If they were acting of their own volition, we could," Season said. "Since they're not, it would mean trying to counter Mother Blessing's influence. I don't know if it'll work."

"It's worth a try, though, right?"

"At this point, anything's worth a try," Season said. She started to add something, but was interrupted by the sound of breaking glass from elsewhere in the house.

"They're coming in!" Kerry breathed.

"Then we have to get out," Season replied. "Kitchen!"

Both women scrambled on hands and knees toward the kitchen entry. From the back door there, a couple of steps led to the small yard, which was overrun by thick shrubbery and low-hanging tree branches. More noise inside the house told Kerry that someone had entered through the bedroom Season slept in, which also had a door facing off to the side of the house. They had no doubt broken one of the panes out of the door and reached in to open it. If they hadn't completely surrounded the house yet, the kitchen door might still be safe.

That was, as Kerry's mother used to say, a pretty big if.

In the kitchen at last, Season once again took the lead. While Kerry hugged the floor, Season looked outside. Not seeing any of the men from her vantage point, she laid out her plan. "I'm going to open this door," she said. "And then I'm going to run like hell for the trees. You give me a couple of seconds, to draw their fire if they're watching, and then follow. We'll meet up at that cliff you climbed."

"All I heard was the run like hell part," Kerry admitted. "And don't worry, that's exactly what I had in mind."

"If they hit me—"

Kerry cut her off. "They won't. Don't even go there."

"I'm just saying—"

The scuff of a foot on the floorboards. "Would you just go, already?" Kerry was afraid she'd have to shove Season out the door.

But Season was already in motion. With a

single smooth move, she swung the door open and launched herself into the darkness outside. Kerry held her breath, expecting the roar of gunfire. Instead she heard the crash of underbrush, and then silence. Fearing the worst—that Season's exit would have alerted the hunters to this way out, even though they had previously been unaware of it—she swallowed once and charged out the door. A patch of light from inside the house floated between her and welcoming darkness, like a wall she would have to penetrate, but she was through it quickly enough and embraced by shadows. Behind her, she heard voices calling out, and then the report of a gun. Leaves not far from her flew as a bullet tore through them, but she kept her head down and ran.

The ground was wet and slick, and branches whipped against Kerry's face and limbs as she ran, snagging fabric and ripping flesh. Not as bad as bullets would, though. She kept running, full out, trying to breathe easily. She knew she was in the best shape of her life—her legs pumped beneath her, each long stride carrying her away from the hunters and the deathtrap their borrowed house had become. As long as she didn't slam herself into a tree trunk in the dark, she would be okay.

Fifteen minutes later she had reached the end of the world.

It might as well have been, at any rate. Of the black Pacific she could see nothing. There were no stars, no moon to be reflected in the water—the clouds overhead blotted out all light. All she could see on the cliff's edge was Season, trying to keep her balance on the rain-slick rocks. Kerry joined her friend there and found cover behind an upthrust boulder, so she couldn't be observed from inland.

Season sat down beside her. Both of them were soaked to the skin, but alive and unhurt. Pneumonia was far easier to fight off than bullets, at least for Kerry.

"Now what?" Kerry asked.

"I hadn't thought that far ahead," Season said. "I just wanted us out of there. Now I guess we hope they give up when they find out the house is empty."

"But they know we were in there," Kerry countered. "They saw us through the window. One of them shot at me when I was running away."

Season shrugged. "I didn't say it was a good plan. Just the best I could come up with at the moment."

"You really think they'll give up?"

"I wouldn't want to count on it," Season admitted, wiping back the hair plastered to her face by the rain. "I guess it depends on how determined Mother Blessing is, and how much control she has over them."

"I have a feeling she's pretty determined."

"I put more hope in the second part, myself," Season said. "If her control over them slips, they'll probably wonder what on Earth they were ever doing out here and head for home."

"That would be good," Kerry said. She allowed herself a flash of optimism, but it didn't last long. "But what if they don't go home? Then we're pretty much trapped here on the cliff."

"Except for one thing," Season pointed out. "We know we can climb down. In this rain they probably can't—especially since they don't have complete control of their own bodies. I'm not saying it would be easy, in this weather, but we could do it. They'll fall for sure."

"And then we'd be killing them anyway," Kerry observed. "Not directly, maybe, but just as dead."

Season contemplated that for a moment. "Yes, that's true. We would be killing them, if you look at it like that."

"So it's not a very good option, is it?"

"I guess not."

They both fell silent then. Kerry tried to think of some other plan, some way to get out of this position. Nothing came to her. They were stuck on a cliff's edge in a driving rain, and armed men were looking for them. Even if they stayed out here all night, there was no guarantee the men would give up. Maybe they'd never give up.

"Kerry . . . ," Season whispered after a time. "I see one of them."

She was peeking around the edge of the sheltering boulder, looking back in the direction of the house.

"Has he seen us?" Kerry asked quietly.

"Not yet," Season answered. "And so far, it's just one of them."

Kerry hazarded a glance of her own. The hunter had broken out of the tree line and was walking toward the cliff, cradling his rifle in his arms and scanning the horizon with every step. Safe behind their boulder, they would be hidden until he was right on top of them. But then it would be a matter of kill or be killed, Kerry was convinced.

"We've got to try something before any more come," she suggested. "Maybe if we pick them off one by one—"

"That's what I was thinking," Season interrupted. "Wait here." She broke from cover and ran toward the man. He reacted to her charge, shouldering the rifle and sighting down it. He moved more slowly than Kerry expected—she guessed that Mother Blessing's remote automation included a built-in time delay, as if some electronic signal had to travel back to her, wherever she was, so she could give the appropriate order.

But Season moved fast, weaving as she ran to make it harder for the sluggish man to draw a bead on her. As he tried, she threw up her hands and shouted "*Takilata!*"

The man stopped dead, as if he'd been struck by a hammer or walked into a brick wall. A look of confusion swept across his face. Season's spell was working!

Kerry's celebration was short-lived, however. The man lowered his gun for a moment, shook off the spell like a man stepping out of a shower, and then raised his weapon again, aiming it right at Season. Kerry stifled a scream as he pulled the trigger. Season hurled herself to the ground, and the bullet whizzed over her head and off to sea.

Hardly losing a moment, Season lunged to her feet and closed the remaining distance between her and the gunman with a fast, zigzag dash. He brought the gun around again, trying to get her in his sights, but his reaction time was too slow. Before he could get off another shot, Season was there. She ducked under the rifle's barrel and slammed it toward the sky with one hand. He managed to squeeze the trigger, but his shot sailed harmlessly toward the clouds. Season braced herself on her left foot and kicked out with her right, catching the man in the gut. He doubled over, and she twisted the rifle from his hands, swinging it around as she did. The rifle's wooden stock collided with the man's jaw, and he crumpled like an empty paper bag.

Season motioned for Kerry to leave cover

and join her. Nervously, afraid to abandon the sheltering rocks, she did so. The man on the ground hadn't moved, and as she approached him, Kerry could see the gleam of dark liquid around his nose and mouth. Blood.

"He's . . . ?"

"He's alive," Season assured her. "But it'll be a little while before he's a problem again. He's just one of them, though, and those two shots will have alerted the others. I think we need to get out of here. This is going to be tougher than I had hoped."

11

Season led Kerry back toward the house by a different, and more roundabout, route than they had taken going out. This was a path Kerry had never seen—didn't even know was here—and it seemed to confirm her guess that while she had been holed up in the house reading, Season had been out scouting something. She should have known it would be escape routes, since they were one of Season's specialties.

"The spell I tried should have paralyzed him," Season whispered as they hurried through the trees. "But it barely slowed him down. Mother Blessing's spell is too deeply embedded for me to break. Our best bet is to deal with them one by one, if they're spread out enough, and make our way to the car.

Chances are she's already overextending herself, so they probably won't be able to follow us any great distance."

"That's encouraging," Kerry replied softly.

"We do the best we can." Season tossed her a wry smile and kept going through the woods.

They met the second of the hunters as they rounded a bend on the trail. He was coming in their direction, shuffling along like a sleepwalker. When he saw the women, though, he seemed to wake up a little. "Over here!" he shouted, bringing his gun up at the same time.

"*Takilata!*" Season tried, making the appropriate hand gestures.

Once again, the man was affected only momentarily. He was so close, however, that Season was able to reach him before he recovered. She cupped both hands over his ears and brought them together hard. The sensation seemed to stun him for another moment, and she followed up with a precisely aimed elbow to his windpipe. He dropped to his knees, choking. Season pushed him over and he fell on the ground, writhing and gasping for breath. She knelt beside him, touching his neck. She looked up at Kerry as she did. "Dislocated his windpipe for a second," she said. "I've fixed it. He'll be fine. But he won't be shouting again soon."

"How did you learn all this stuff?" Kerry inquired.

"Here and there," Season said vaguely. Kerry took the hint and let it drop.

Leaving him moaning softly on the wet path, they continued toward the house. Rustling nearby indicated that the man's initial cry had not gone unheard. Season gestured to Kerry and they both left the path, taking to the trees and waiting, as still as possible, a couple of feet back.

Less than a minute later, two of the hunters came down the path, stiff-legged and awkward. Their guns were at the ready, but their eyes were only on the trail. They walked right past Season and Kerry without ever noticing them standing among the trees. The women waited another couple of minutes, until they could no longer hear the two men, and then took to the path again.

They were almost back to the house when they encountered yet another of the hunters.

Season braced herself for action, but Kerry put a restraining hand on her arm. "Let me try something," she said.

Season looked surprised, but then smiled. "Be my guest."

Kerry waited until the guy had spotted them and prepared to sound the alarm, and then she folded the fingers of her right hand until the fingertips touched the palm, and extended her thumb. With her left hand, she made a lifting motion. "*Kenesep!*" she exclaimed.

The man's cry died in his throat as a plume of earth rose up and hurled itself into his face. He backpedaled away from it, but his impaired control over his own limbs got in the way and he fell over backward, smacking his head against a tree stump with an audible crack. He rolled to the ground and lay still.

"You don't think I broke anything, do you?" Kerry asked, suddenly worried that she'd taken it too far.

"I doubt it," Season answered. Dropping to one knee beside the man, she examined the back of his head briefly. "I think he just got knocked out. Come on."

The 4x4 they had bought in San Francisco was parked within view, and there were no hunters readily apparent. They broke into a sprint. Kerry knew they'd left their purses, driver's licenses and all, back in the house, and probably their keys as well.

She also knew that wouldn't matter—such inconveniences were easily fixed with the help of a little witchcraft.

Season hit the driver's side door and yanked it open. Kerry ran around to the passenger side, and by the time she was in her seat, Season was already backing out of the gravel driveway. Kerry buckled in just as Season straightened out on the dirt road and stomped on the gas.

Some of the hunters heard the sounds of the vehicle and came running—running, at least, to the extent that their slow-moving bodies would allow. A couple of them raised their rifles, and Kerry heard shots fired behind them. No bullets impacted the Raider, however. Within minutes she and Season had left them far behind, cutting through the rain toward the highway out of Bolinas.

• • •

Mother Blessing knew when her targets were out of range. During the search and battle, she had taken refuge in a cheap motel room on the San Francisco peninsula, directing the action from there since she couldn't both drive and participate. Trucks rumbling past threatened to disturb her concentration, but she tuned the room's TV to a channel it didn't receive and cranked the volume, letting the white noise drown out traffic sounds from outside. Watching through multiple pairs of eyes—and eyes she had not manufactured, but only enchanted—was a strain in itself; doing that and controlling muscles, planning and executing strategy, took a lot out of a person. And now she knew that Season and Kerry were headed north—toward the Convocation site, no doubt—and that her plan had not worked.

Still, she'd had to try. The Convocation was upon them. Season could have decided to leave at any minute. Since she couldn't make it to Bolinas herself in a timely enough fashion, she had stopped in this motel and used its telephone book to locate a gun shop in Marin County, not too far from Bolinas. She then constructed a simulacrum and sent it into the shop, watching through its eyes to see who was inside. There were half a dozen men, some dressed like they were ready for the hunt, others engaged in conversation, shopping, or just browsing.

She didn't care why they had gone in, only that they were there.

It was brutally difficult—almost impossible, really—to cast spells over long distances. But the distance in this case wasn't too extreme, less than fifty miles, and she had the help of the simulacrum, whose hands could be sculpted into the precise necessary shapes for limited durations. She cast an overall spell on the men in the shop, freezing them where they stood, and then spent more time enchanting each one individually. She drilled the address of Rebecca's friends, the Morgans, into them, showed them their targets, and sent them on their way.

If that first shot had hit Kerry, she'd have had them both. Season wouldn't have abandoned the girl. She would have been so angry that she would have waited for Mother Blessing to arrive, just so she could have it out with her. Mother Blessing chuckled dryly.

Human emotion could be so counterproductive, and Season had never been able to completely shake that handicap.

As it turned out, though the man she had used for the first attack had been the most seasoned hunter of the lot, her own manipulation of him had affected his ability to aim cleanly and to squeeze off a good shot.

Not for the first time, she wished she could have been there in person. All the distance Season kept between them had kept her alive too many times. Mother Blessing was grimly aware that she had not been able to best Season the last time they'd been face-to-face, but that was then.

This was now. She was ready this time. She was primed. She had been preparing, training, learning.

All she needed was to meet up with Season Howe, one-on-one.

It peeved her royally to realize that it probably wasn't going to happen. Season had too much of a start. She was already racing toward the Convocation, while Mother Blessing tried to recover from a difficult, and ultimately futile, exercise. Perhaps she had, in fact, compounded her earlier mistake by going with surrogates yet again. If she had just driven straight to Bolinas, it was possible that Season and Kerry would have still been there, would have waited until morning to make the drive north.

But now she had flushed them out, and they were on the wing again. Even if Mother Blessing got on the road right now, Season had a couple of hours' head start. Mother Blessing's only hope was to drive through San Francisco, over the Golden Gate Bridge, and onto Interstate 80. From where Season was, she'd have a long haul to get to the Interstate, looping over the north end of the San Francisco Bay. Their way would be slow. It was remotely possible that Mother Blessing would be able to intercept them before they reached the Convocation, if she hurried. Maybe in Sacramento.

Leaving the TV blaring its noisy signal, Mother Blessing dragged herself wearily to her car.

Season pulled the car to a stop outside a twenty-four-hour family restaurant near Richmond. She had watched the mirror constantly since leaving Bolinas, and there had been no pursuit. She and Kerry were both hungry, and if they were going to drive all night they'd need some nourishment, and probably caffeine. This place would be quiet at this time of night, she explained. They'd be able to scrutinize all the diners at a glance as soon as they went in, and if anyone looked suspicious or made a move against them, they could immediately retreat or fight back.

Before they went in, Kerry pulled her cell phone from the purse that Season had magically arranged to be inside the car. *Either that,* Kerry thought, *or the purse is an exact duplicate of my old one, right down to the last stick of gum in its wrapper and the programming on the phone.* Only the names on her driver's license and credit cards were changed—now, as far as the public was concerned, she was Brenda Peterson, and Season was Amanda Cowles.

"I need to call Beck," she said. "I've been really worried about her."

"That's fine," Season said. "I think we're safe for the moment."

Season punched up Rebecca's home number. The phone rang only once before someone snatched it from the cradle on the other end. "Hello?" the voice asked breathlessly. Kerry recognized it at once, but it wasn't who she wanted to talk to.

"Erin?" Kerry said. "It's Kerry. Is Rebecca there?"

"God, no," Erin said. She sounded distraught. "I was hoping you were her."

"No, sorry. Where is she?"

"That's the thing, Kerry. I don't know. Scott and, what's her name, Brandy, were calling and calling, like, all night last night. They stopped for a while this morning, but they've been back at it now and then. I'm really worried about her. She left me a note saying she was leaving for a day or so, and that's the last anyone seems to have heard from her."

Kerry's heart sank. The bad feeling she'd had about Rebecca was accurate, and then some. Unfortunately, it didn't take an advanced degree in mathematics to put the puzzle pieces together. *Rebecca knew where we were,* she thought. *Rebecca vanishes, Mother Blessing turns up. Not a complicated pattern.*

"Okay, Erin," she said. "If you hear from her, please have her call me right away. I'll have her check in with you if I can reach her."

"Thanks, Kerry," Erin said. She sniffled, and Kerry guessed that she had started to weep. Sometimes the two housemates seemed barely aware of one another's existence, but that arrangement had worked for them. Rebecca even seemed to prefer it, since it made it easier to keep important aspects of her life private. But Erin genuinely liked Rebecca, in her own way. Of course she'd be worried and upset.

Kerry ended the call and turned to Season. "Rebecca's missing," she said. "Since last night sometime."

"Plenty of time for Mother Blessing to have found us," Season said, catching on instantly.

The ease with which Season jumped to the same conclusion that she had chilled Kerry to the bone. "That's what I was thinking."

"Try the others," Season urged. "Make sure they're okay."

Kerry was already scrolling for Scott's number. She prepared to call it, but at the last second changed her mind and chose Brandy's instead. She knew those two had had their troubles, and she knew that she was at the root of at least some of it. Why make things worse by always calling Scott first, instead of Brandy?

"Kerry?" Brandy answered a moment later.

"Hi, Brandy." Kerry didn't have time for pleasantries. "Have you heard from Rebecca?"

"No, we haven't been able to reach her all day," Brandy said. "Have you?"

"I just now talked to Erin and found out she was missing. I didn't know. Erin said she was going out of town for a while but didn't seem to know much more than that."

"It gets worse," Brandy told her. Kerry almost pulled the phone away from her head, afraid to hear what Brandy might have to say now.

"What?" she asked, almost against her own will.

"Adam was attacked," Brandy said. "By a simulacrum. Scott and I managed to fight it off—well, Scott did really. It was like some kind of miracle, Kerry—the thing just fell apart in his hands. But that was yesterday. We wanted to let you know Mother Blessing was on the move again, so we tried to call you. But when we couldn't get you, we called Rebecca.

She said she would go to wherever you are and find you, warn you that something was up."

"Oh, no," Kerry said, as the weight of Brandy's words sank in.

"Yeah."

"Brandy, Rebecca never showed up, but some goons under Mother Blessing's control did."

"And Rebecca's the only one who knew where you were."

"Yeah," Kerry echoed Brandy. "I didn't want to tell Erin, but I'm really worried about her."

"Sounds like you have reason to be," Brandy said. "I kept hoping maybe she was with you, and you were all out of cell range or something."

"No such luck," Kerry said. "I wish."

"Me too."

Both were silent for a moment. Kerry thought she was going to cry, like Erin had. Only with more reason.

"I should tell Scott," Brandy said.

"Is he with you?"

"Yeah," Brandy said. "We're in a rental car,

on our way to Santa Cruz. We landed at the airport in San Jose about a half hour ago—first flight out of Boston we were able to get."

"You guys be careful," Kerry urged, surprised to learn that they were already in California. "Chances are Mother Blessing is on her way up here, heading for the Convocation. But if she is still in Santa Cruz, I don't need to tell you she's very dangerous."

"I know, Kerry," Brandy said. "We won't take any stupid chances. But what if Rebecca is, I don't know, trapped someplace and needs our help? We have to look for her."

"You do that. I'll see if Season knows a way to search for her remotely. When you've found her, or . . . or when you're ready, head north, to Oregon." She drew the phone away from her mouth. "Where should they meet us, Season? After?"

"Have them wait in Klamath Falls," Season said. "That's not too far, and there are motels they can stay at."

"Klamath Falls, Season says," Kerry spoke into the phone. "I'll call you when I can to find out where you are. The Witches' Convocation is about to start, but we'll hook up with you after that. And everything will be different then, I can guarantee it."

"Everything's already different," Brandy said. "That doesn't mean I have to like it."

"Yeah," Kerry agreed. "That's a really good point."

12

It felt to Kerry as if they'd left the world behind.

She had never been anywhere so desolate, so isolated. Even the Great Dismal Swamp had been teeming with life, and there had been people around, towns all around it.

Not here, though. None of that.

She and Season had traded off at the wheel of the Dodge Raider through the night. They had bisected California on Interstate 80, leaving city and suburbs behind, entering agricultural areas, then the soupy region of the Sacramento Delta. Sacramento came and went in the dark, and once again they could smell rich and fertile farmlands surrounding them. Then the road started to climb. Flat fields turned to foothills, alfalfa and sugar beets to pines and firs and towering redwoods that blotted out the stars.

They had stopped for a few hours in Truckee, checking into a motel and grabbing some much-needed sleep on top of matching twin beds without even bothering to pull down the bedding. Breakfast was had at lunchtime in a nearby café, and then they were back in the car. The highway left California behind as it wove down from the mountains—the same Sierra Nevadas, Kerry reflected, that Season had mentioned earlier in her diatribe about global warming. That had been an eon ago, though, another age, before people had started shooting at them.

Coming down out of the mountains, they drove into Reno, which jutted up from the relative flatland like a child's toy forgotten on a lawn. Soon enough, even Reno vanished in the rearview mirror, and with it anything that smacked of population. The highway turned to the north and sliced through a state that seemed utterly abandoned. Every now and then there would be a roadside gas station/store/restaurant, or the buildings of some distant ranch, and then nothing again but mile after mile of rolling plains of sagebrush.

Then Winnemucca, a blink of the eye, and Season, who refused to reveal their destination except as the site of the Convocation, surprised Kerry by turning off Interstate 80 altogether.

Now she drove due north on Highway 95, a narrow strip of roadway that barely deserved the dignity of being numbered. It was paved, Kerry reflected, but that was about all it had going for it. With the setting sun on Season's side of the car, they drove up and up. There were mountains looming in the distance—this was basin and range country, Season had explained, which meant relatively parallel mountain ranges separated by deep valleys, like the wales of corduroy, cutting across the landscape. They followed the roadway through one of the valleys. Then the sun dropped behind the mountains to the west, and Season pulled over to let Kerry take the wheel for a stretch.

"Where are we?" Kerry wanted to know.

"Right here." This was about the extent that Season had been willing to reveal for hours.

"And where are we going?"

Season ticked her head north, on up the road. "That way."

Kerry blew out a frustrated sigh. "Okay. Will I know when we get there?"

"You'll know," Season promised her. "You will definitely know."

Kerry drove on, into the gathering dusk. There were no lights to be seen anywhere. If anyone actually lived out here, she couldn't tell. The idea suddenly struck her that this would be an awfully remote place to run out of gas, but then she smiled at her own naïveté—they hadn't stopped for gas since they'd bought the vehicle, and they wouldn't have to.

Finally, as stars began to wink into sight in the darkening sky, Season touched her right arm.

"Slow down," she said.

"Okay." Kerry complied. "Are we looking for something?"

"We are," Season confirmed. Kerry continued up the road for a couple of miles, with Season eyeing the left shoulder. Finally, she touched Kerry's arm once again. "We're looking for that."

Kerry followed her pointing hand. Season seemed to be pointing to a narrow, rutted track that led away from the highway. "That . . . that little path?"

"That's right," Season said. "Take that."

"This thing will be okay on that road? Is that really a road?"

Season showed her how to shift the Raider into its four-wheel drive mode. "This thing can go anywhere," she promised. "Just don't go too fast if you don't have to. Slow and easy."

Kerry almost asked why she might have to go fast, if slow was preferred, but then decided she'd rather not know. With Rebecca missing and Mother Blessing on the warpath, she had enough troubles weighing on her mind as it was. She turned onto the little track. The Raider chewed up the road easily, and she increased its pace a little, learning to slow down when approaching bumps or hollows. The headlights illuminated bugs flitting past, occasional clumps of sagebrush, dirt, and not much else. Once a pair of pronghorns dashed across a hill, limned against the rising moon.

A couple of hours later, Kerry yawned and

stretched, gripping the wheel with one hand while she pushed the other against the ceiling, then trading off. "We're almost there," Season assured her. "Not much farther."

Kerry looked out into the distance and realized that beyond the headlights she couldn't see anything at all. The moon seemed to shine down on absolute nothingness.

"Are we still in Nevada?" she asked. "Are we still on Earth?"

"We may have passed into Oregon," Season told her. "I'm not a hundred percent sure about that. But don't worry, we're just about there."

Kerry brought the 4X4 to a shuddering stop and stared at Season as if the woman had gone insane. "Almost where? We're nowhere! There's nothing here. No one. Nada." She shut off the headlights and got out of the vehicle. She hadn't realized it, so focused was she on the narrow cone that the headlights illuminated, but they had been driving for some time on a perfectly flat, perfectly empty stretch of land. Beneath her feet, the hardpan was baked solid, the dirt cracked in hexagonal shapes. It looked like brownies left in the oven too long.

She spun around, indicating the field of nothingness with her hands.

With the headlights gone, the moon shone down on the vast, empty space, which seemed to glow whitely of its own volition. Overhead, against the black backdrop of night, Kerry thought she could see every star there had ever been. The white sweep of the Milky Way had never been so distinct.

Season walked over to her, her boots crunching on the crusted earth. "Feel better?" she asked sympathetically.

"I'll feel better when I know where we are," Kerry groused.

"We're in the Owyhee Desert," Season told her. "It crosses between northern Nevada and southern Oregon. A lot of maps don't bother to name it, because what's the point? There's nothing here."

"A whole lot of nothing," Kerry said. "I can see that much."

"I mean, real nothing," Season said. "This is one of the emptiest spots in the United States. The population density of Humboldt County, Nevada, which we just passed through, is somewhere less than two people per square mile, and most of those live back down in Winnemucca. Here it's probably figured in negative numbers."

"Meaning what?"

"Meaning there are more dead people than living, around here."

"That's a comforting thought," Kerry said.

"It's just empty," Season said. "Nothing wrong with that. It's what we're looking for."

"It is?"

"I'll show you," Season offered. "Get back in."

Kerry grudgingly complied. She had come to trust Season, but she didn't like how secretive her mentor had been about this whole thing. She could probably backtrack and return to civilization if she needed to, but only because there were so few roads that it would be hard to get genuinely lost.

But she got in and buckled up, with Season taking the wheel again. The older witch started the engine, flicked on the headlights, and began driving up the dirt trail, faster than Kerry had done.

"We're really someplace?" Kerry asked. "This is like some kind of weird hallucination."

Season chuckled. "That's it exactly," she

said. "Don't see what your eyes tell you to see."

"Sometimes you are so opaque," Kerry commented. "Why don't you just say what you mean?"

"Don't see dark, flat, empty land," Season pressed. "Close your eyes and see the Convocation."

"How can I? I don't even know what it looks like. But if it looks like this, I'm going to be seriously bummed."

"It looks like a carnival," Season told her. "Not a modern one. Maybe a medieval one. Look at the peaked tents—blue, white, red, yellow, green. Look at the banners and pennants fluttering from their points, at the bright piping wrapped around their guy lines, like garlands around the staircase at Christmas. Look at the little wooden buildings where people serve food and drink, and the fires roaring in the wind, sprays of sparks dancing up into the sky, where they cook the beef and ham and turkey, and the smaller fires where they grill the vegetables. Smell the aromatic smoke that funnels up like dust devils. Look at the people walking between the tents and the buildings, chatting and laughing and enjoying being in one another's company again, safe and at home. See the dance floor, encircled by glowing paper lanterns, where couples in their most elegant finery twirl to the music provided by the band in the little frame gazebo."

Kerry realized that she *could* see the things Season described as the Raider bounced its way across the blank lunar landscape. It was just because her eyes were shut, and Season's words were so hypnotic, so evocative, she knew.

But no! Her eyes were wide open. Somehow, as if they had passed through an invisible curtain, they were now driving toward something, instead of toward more of the same nothing. It was just as Season had described it—she hadn't been imagining it after all, she had been stating what she was seeing, right in front of her. The tall tents with fluttering flags, the fires, the crowded dance floor.

And most of all, the people.

The witches.

Kerry Profitt's diary, March 21.

I'm home.

I've never been home before. Not really. Well,

okay, maybe when I was a little kid and both of my parents were alive, back in Cairo where I was born and bred. But not since then. Certainly not since Mom passed on and I had to move in with my aunt and uncle.

But I'm home now. I felt it as soon as I could truly see the Convocation, as soon as Season's words turned into reality for me.

If you weren't meant to be here, you would never see it. If for some bizarre reason you were driving on that goddess-awful dirt road and you weren't a witch, you'd just keep driving right through, never realizing that you had just missed the greatest celebration you could ever have imagined.

I'm meant to be here, then, because I can see it, and smell it, and hear it. Season and I are staying inside one of the little wooden caravans, like an old-time gypsy's, or a carny's, and every now and then I just have to get up and go to the door and stare outside at everyone and everything. Kind of like pinching myself to make sure I'm not dreaming, only without the pinch part.

It's amazing. Everyone is so happy, so friendly. Smiling. Laughing. Shouting to people they haven't seen in . . . well, in five hundred years. Calling to each other, running together, hugging. Lots of hugging.

And the sounds are so musical, so enchanting. The smells are heavenly. The clothes are . . . everything. Outfits from every time period in the last five centuries, and from every part of the world, but they all mesh together, they all blend perfectly, and they are all beautiful—the finest fabrics, the most skilled workmanship. I felt like a grunge in my dirty T-shirt and jeans and red-checked tennies, but then I looked down at myself, and my clothes seemed to have a glow to them. Same clothes, but somehow they had become fitting and appropriate and perfect, just like everyone else's. Every skin color on Earth is represented, too, and just like the clothes, it all makes a glorious visual display.

It's the world's biggest, best party. That's the only real way to describe it. A party where everybody likes each other, and no one is obnoxiously drunk or hitting on someone who doesn't want to be hit on.

It's a celebration of witchiness. It's a gala. It's a convention. It's a business meeting. It's a dream.

It's the Convocation.

It's home.

Somebody pinch me after all. Or don't, on

second thought, because I don't want to wake up from this.

More later.

K.

13

When Brandy and Scott got to Rebecca's house in Santa Cruz, the place was crawling with police. Rebecca's VW was parked across the street, with yellow police tape surrounding it and the area immediately around it. Arc lights on tall stanchions gave a surreally bright glow to jumpsuited officers with cameras and evidence kits. It looked like a CSI episode come horribly to life, since it brought home with cruel bluntness the fact that Rebecca was truly missing.

At the door to the house, they had to introduce themselves to a sympathetic but terse female officer, who then announced them to Erin. Erin immediately rushed to the door to let them in. They had never met her, but Brandy recognized her from Rebecca's descriptions and a couple of photos. She was the archetypal California blonde—petite, button-cute, hair pulled back into a bouncy ponytail. But her red nose and the dark circles around her puffy eyes showed that she was not always the epitome of perk.

She led them into the kitchen. Brandy could hear cops moving in other parts of the house, and the static and buzz of their two-way radios. The kitchen was mercifully empty of them, and Erin sat down at a vintage Formica-topped table, in front of a cup of tea that looked like it had been there awhile.

"I'm so sorry I, you know, hung up on you guys," she said sadly. "I . . . you know, I thought she was just out or whatever, and you were just getting on my nerves. But if I had known . . ."

"How could you?" Brandy asked, pulling out a chair of her own and joining Erin at the table. "Her note said that she was going away for some indefinite period of time. So when she did just that, you had no reason to think there was anything wrong."

"Yeah, I guess so," Erin agreed as tears began to roll down her cheeks. "But still . . . there must have been something I missed.

Some clue. I should have noticed sooner that her car was still there."

"You can't beat yourself up too much," Scott told her. He had remained standing, scanning the kitchen as if there might be a clue everyone else had missed. "Whatever happened to her is not your fault, I know that."

Brandy reflected that he couldn't tell Erin why he knew it. Erin had no inkling, she was certain, of the existence of Season Howe and Mother Blessing and the whole long war between them. Rebecca had sworn that she would never tell anyone outside of their circle—those who had been living in the La Jolla house the night they found Daniel Blessing, half dead, in the shrubbery outside. The night it all began. Brandy had never had occasion to think Rebecca anything less than scrupulously honest—if she made a promise, she kept it.

She almost wished she could say something now. If Erin could know what her housemate was really caught up in, it would lessen any feelings of guilt she might have over Rebecca's disappearance. But Brandy held her tongue. Erin was so emotionally vulnerable right now, so close to the edge, that she would either think Brandy was a complete, unabashed liar, or she would believe the story, realize that the entire framework of knowledge she had about the world was wrong, and go totally insane.

The La Jolla housemates had at least had some time to get used to the existence of witches, and the knowledge had been thrust on them at a time when they were relatively happy, secure, and comfortable with each other. Erin had no such advantages. She would be knocked over at her weakest point, and her grip on reality might not survive it.

So instead of telling her the only thing that might really ease her pain, Brandy took Erin's hand and gently rubbed the back of it. "He's right," she said. "It's not your fault, Erin. We'll look for her. She's probably fine."

Only, of course, she probably wasn't. Mother Blessing had located Kerry and Season. Only Rebecca could have told her where to look. Unless she had come across the information some other way, Rebecca was certainly in serious trouble.

Behind her, Brandy heard Scott walking around, and then he left the kitchen altogether.

She glanced at Erin and they both fell silent, listening as he addressed a police officer they couldn't see.

"Can you tell me anything about the investigation?" he asked. "We're close friends of Rebecca's—we actually just flew in from Boston to see her, and if there's anything we can do to help we'd really like to know."

"The best I can tell you is to keep out of the way and let us handle it," the police officer replied, his tone sympathetic but firm. "We can do our jobs."

"I know," Scott pressed. "But have you, you know, checked the hospitals and stuff? In case she's been in an accident or something?"

"We're working on it, son," the officer said. "Like I said—"

"I didn't mean to imply that you weren't," Scott said, cutting him off. "I just figured, if there was something we could do that would take some of the pressure off you, we'd be happy to."

"If I think of anything, I'll let you know," the officer said. Brandy heard the jangle of equipment on his belt as he walked away, and then Scott came back into the kitchen.

"They've got nothing," he said. "They're never going to find her."

The cops had nothing, but Brandy and Scott had no clue where to look for her either. The reality of it loomed over Brandy like a falling piano. Soon enough, the piano would hit.

"I've been missin' y'all."

Kerry was not surprised to hear Mother Blessing's voice, or to see her when she spun around at the sound of it. Season had assured her that their enemy would be in attendance. She also swore that Mother Blessing would be polite, even friendly, on the grounds of the Convocation, but Kerry tensed just the same, ready to run or fight.

Mother Blessing stood a dozen feet behind them, supporting her weight on a black metal cane. Even her usual polyester stretch pants and tentlike top seemed enhanced by their presence here, looking more like the garb of some weird kind of royalty than like the discount store specials they usually resembled.

"*Barely* missing," Season added.

Mother Blessing's smile broadened. "Well, a lady has to try, right? I thought maybe I'd run into y'all in Sacramento, but somehow you got past me."

"Imagine that," Season replied, returning the woman's ghastly grin. "I hope you didn't injure any innocent civilians while you were looking for us."

Mother Blessing laughed uproariously, as if Season had just told the best joke ever. Kerry couldn't quite get over these mortal enemies acting like old friends. She was reminded of politicians shaking hands before a debate, calling each other liars and cheats for an hour, and then shaking again when it was all over.

Then the old witch focused her gaze on Kerry, who twitched uncertainly beneath it. "Hope y'all are well, Kerry," she said. "It's been awful lonely at home since you left."

"Yeah, I bet you really wish I was back there," Kerry said, not bothering to hide the sarcastic edge. She was no politician, and she didn't intend to behave like one.

Season poked Kerry in the ribs, covering the action by laughing and grabbing Kerry's arm. "Kerry's told me all about how much she's learned from you, daughter," she said. It freaked Kerry out to be reminded that the youthful Season Howe was, in fact, Mother Blessing's mother. "I'm surprised that you turned out to be such a good teacher."

"Kerry's a good pupil," Mother Blessing answered. "A natural."

"That's true," Season said. "I guess you have an eye for them."

"I like to think so."

"We were just on our way to get some breakfast," Season said, bringing the uncomfortable conversation to a diplomatic close. "Would you like to join us?"

Kerry wanted to poke Season this time, but her friend had moved out of reach. Fortunately, Mother Blessing politely declined the offer.

Walking through the golden sunshine toward a tent from which wafted a glorious assortment of aromas, Kerry fixed Season with a curious glare. "What was all that about?"

"It won't do us any good to get into a brawl here," Season answered reasonably. "We're at the Convocation. No one's getting hurt now. Nothing's going to happen until Witches' Tribunal, and then it'll be under the procedures that have been in place for centuries. If she was going to kill us, she needed to do it before we got here. Now we're perfectly safe from her."

Kerry couldn't quite wrap her mind around that idea. Perfectly safe? There had been a time in her life when she had felt safe, but not in the last year or so. She had been on edge virtually every minute, starting at every unusual noise, eyeing strangers with suspicion. She supposed that maybe she would be able to fully relax again someday.

It would take a while, though.

Regardless of Season's assurances, she would not trust Mother Blessing until after the Witches' Tribunal had dealt out its justice.

The breakfast offered in the tent was every bit as delicious as its odors promised. A crew of chefs in restaurant whites with tall hats—but all decorated with a wide assortment of cheerful buttons, braids, tassels, patches, and other additions, and all working with uniform good cheer—turned out an equally wide assortment of dishes. There were omelets and eggs of every style, various meats and sausages, pancakes and waffles, cereals, pastries, fruits. . . . Kerry could barely bring herself to pick anything, because it all looked so good.

"No wonder you cook so well," she said to Season as they examined their options. "Do witches always eat like this?"

"Sometimes it's gruel and hardtack," Season teased. "But what's the point of having a party if you can't indulge yourself?"

They filled plates and then sat down at long tables. The benches were filled with witches chatting, laughing, and seeming to have a good time. There were more women than men, but not by a huge margin. Kerry and Season squeezed in at the end of one of the benches, where a couple of people moved over to make space for them. Season hugged them both, a man and a woman.

"It's so good to see you," she gushed. "Kerry, this is Horace and Mae. They're witches from—Wisconsin, is it?"

"Madison," Horace said, beaming at Kerry like they were long-lost pals. He was as lean as a greyhound, with thinning silver hair combed over a bald spot, and small-lensed wire-rim glasses perched on a prominent nose. He could have been sixty or, Kerry knew, six hundred. Mae was rounder, more heavyset, with grandmotherly gray curls and a pearl chain attached to her horn-rims. Both were dressed like the grandparents in one of those black-and-white TV sitcoms from the fifties that ran on TV late at night.

"I've been to Madison!" Kerry said excitedly. The giddy mood of the other diners was infecting her. "Last fall, on my way down . . . down south."

"You've got to be pretty far north for Madison to be on the way south," Mae observed with a giggle.

"I figured that out," Kerry replied. She had realized that she didn't want to get carried away and reveal that she'd been on her way to stay with Mother Blessing. Everybody acted friendly here, but that didn't mean there weren't factions, and she wanted to be cautious about saying too much to the wrong person. At least until she could get the lay of the land, or find out from Season who to trust. "I didn't exactly take the most direct route."

"Did you like it, Kerry?" Horace asked.

"I really didn't stay long," Kerry admitted. "It was cold, mostly. That's what I remember."

"Well, you should come back this time of

year. Between now and early summer. It's a real nice place."

"It looked like it," Kerry said. "I'd like to go back sometime."

"I met Horace and Mae in . . . what was it, 1890?" Season asked.

"Ninety-one, I think," Mae corrected. "That winter."

"They helped me out of a tight spot," Season continued. "They're good folks." Kerry waited for her to elaborate further, but she didn't. Instead she dug into her breakfast with gusto. Kerry followed her lead and did the same, not wanting to let it get cold.

After breakfast Season introduced her to another dozen or so old friends as they wandered through the lanes between tents, pavilions, and small wooden buildings. In these, every kind of witchy activity Kerry could imagine took place. Some held demonstrations of spells or potions. Some were shops where magical implements—swords, daggers, wands, cauldrons, herbs, censers, brooms, crystals, and more—were displayed and traded. Everything within the Convocation grounds seemed to be bathed in a soft, gentle glow. Kerry had thought at first it was just early morning light slanting down on things, but as the day wore on, it didn't dissipate or change. Finally, she asked Season about it.

"It's the light of magic," Season said. "Sometimes you'll hear late afternoon, just a little before sunset, when the sun is at an angle and the light has a golden tinge, referred to as the 'magic hour.' And that's by civilians. They don't know how close they are to the truth, but somehow the truth has filtered down to them."

Kerry didn't understand. "But . . ." She couldn't even come up with the question.

Season got it, though. "It's all around us. This whole thing, the Convocation. Remember the desert outside here? Flat, dry, hot, empty? We are here, we're not an illusion. But to an outsider, we wouldn't be. It's magic. We are bathed in it here, suffused in it. Those pavilions, those chairs, those trailers . . . they weren't here two days ago, and they won't be here next week. Not in the sense that one typically thinks of as 'here.' The molecules that make them up will be returned to where they came from—around here, pretty much dirt, and maybe a few scrubby sagebrush bushes for texture."

"But I don't see a glow like that when I cast a spell," Kerry pressed.

"Because a spell is an isolated instance of magic," Season explained. "Transitory, only there for the moment. Here there's nothing isolated about it. It's as much a part of our environment as the air itself. It would be strange if there *wasn't* an optical manifestation of it."

Good enough for me, Kerry thought. *That explains why my cruddy jeans and T-shirts look so spiff, and Mother Blessing's nightmare wardrobe too. Probably why everyone's in such a good mood, too.* For her part, Kerry felt better than she had in ages—years, maybe. Not just physically, but emotionally. She felt like she was in the bosom of a large, extended family, surrounded by people who cared about her, even though in fact most of them had never met or heard about her. But everyone Season introduced her to greeted her happily. She had never been made so welcome anywhere in her life.

For the morning, she and Season had no particular schedule, no appointments to keep.

They just wandered, taking in the sights and sounds. Kerry tried to estimate the size of the Convocation, or the attendance, but found that it was impossible. Sometimes she thought they were almost at the end of a row, but then they would go into a tent or a shop, and when they emerged the row would stretch out toward the horizon, the empty desert she thought she had glimpsed totally eclipsed by light and color and activity. Every now and then she got the feeling that things were changing right behind them—like if they went into one stall, the one they had just left would metamorphose into something entirely different, so that one could never experience the whole array.

An astonishing variety of blooming flowers edged the paths and filled in spaces between the tents and buildings, a carpet of reds, whites, oranges, pinks, yellows, violets, and greens. Considering what she knew the "real" landscape around her looked like, Kerry was especially delighted to see the displays of poppies and daisies, lupines and lilacs, sunflowers and sacred datura.

Only one thing nagged at her, keeping her happiness from being complete. She remembered how much Daniel had looked forward to his first Convocation. He had told her stories of past ones—like Season and her daughter, he'd never been but he was full of the tales that witches handed down to one another. She couldn't help wishing it was Daniel walking beside her now. Maybe even him and Season, both having learned that they weren't one another's real enemy. Daniel's large, warm hand enveloping hers, his ready smile, his clear gray eyes crinkling in the golden magic-light. That would have made this experience perfect.

That afternoon she and Season took part in a ritual with about a thousand other witches.

With no verbal communication of which Kerry was aware, no printed schedule or loud-speaker announcement or anything like that, everyone seemed to just filter toward a vast, empty, grassy meadow that she would have sworn hadn't been there before.

Kerry wore a simple white shift that she'd picked up in one of the shops, which she learned were "shops" only in name, since they accepted no payment for the merchandise they provided. Her feet were bare. On her head was a wreath of fresh spring flowers: greens, whites, pale yellows. Ribbons streamed down her back, entwining with her long, silken black hair. She had no makeup on, but she felt beautiful without it. Not that she had done more than glance into a mirror to make sure the wreath was on straight since she had arrived at the Convocation—the beauty she felt was of the spirit, not the flesh. It was a sense of peace, of belonging.

With Season at her side, and with hundreds of other witches joining them, she walked down a gentle slope toward the meadow, as if she just knew it was where she was supposed to be. Some of the witches spoke in hushed, almost reverent tones, but here the mood seemed different than it had up on the hill. This was a special place, a sacred place, and the sometimes rowdy, raucous good humor of the Convocation's public spaces was left behind. In its place was a more spiritual, but equally comfortable, atmosphere.

In the meadow, the witches formed naturally into a great circle. Three witches, two women and a man, stood at the center of the circle, gathered about an altar of upthrust stones that looked like it had been there for a thousand years. On the ancient altar were a spray of flowers and branches, a cauldron also filled with flowers, a fat red candle, a knife, and a censer. When all the witches were gathered— and Kerry didn't know how the ones at the center knew that no more were coming, but they seemed to—one of them lit incense in the censer, and then lit the candle. Flame leaped up from each, then settled to a steady glow.

One of the women at the front lifted the knife and held it in the smoke from the censer for a second. Her hair was waist length and silver, hanging in thick braids around her, and her skin, though lined, looked as fresh as a child's. She smiled out at the gathering, turning in a slow circle so everyone could see the knife. Then she put its point down into the cauldron and said, "I consecrate and cleanse this water, that it may be purified and fit to dwell within this circle of our love. In the name of the Goddess and the God, the Mother and the Father, I consecrate this water."

That said, she lifted the knife from the

cauldron, and Kerry saw that its blade was wet. There was water in the cauldron, then, with the flowers inside it sticking out as if from a vase. The man, tall and dark, with a heavy brow and huge hands, stepped to the cauldron next, and dipped his fingers into the water. He turned to the north and dribbled some of the water in that direction. Then he dipped his hand again, and repeated the process to the east, south, and west.

Preparations finished, the third witch took her place at the altar. This one was younger than the others, her blond hair almost white in the sunshine. She put her hands in the flowers, both the ones laying across the altar and the ones in the cauldron, and said, "O great Goddess, you have thrown off the icy grip of winter and embraced the warmth of spring. Now is the greening, the rebirth, the renewal. All things begin again, life takes root in all ways, in the germination and sprouting of every seed, in each breeze that bears warmth on its shoulders, in each ray of sunlight that falls upon your earth."

All three of the witches at the altar joined hands, and as one, the witches in attendance did as well. Everyone in the crowd, at least a thousand strong, was connected to everyone else. The witches at the altar began to speak, and the ones in the audience said the words along with them. Even Kerry knew what to say, as if reading from an invisible script.

"We walk the earth in kinship, in friendship, not in dominance. We are one with the trees and flowers in the field, one with the rocks and hills and mountains, one with each drop of water in the oceans and each grain of sand in the deserts. We are one with all the creatures on, beneath, and above the earth and her oceans. We ask not permission to use the earth but to exist with the earth, in harmony and cooperation with the Goddess and all she represents. We pledge in return to adore and appreciate her clean skies, her fresh rivers, the green and abundant bounty of her skin."

Even as she spoke the words, holding Season's hand in her left and a stranger's in her right, feeling the power of the thousand flowing through her like an electric charge, Kerry thought she could see minuscule green sparks rising up from the candle like motes of pollen. They rose until they were above the crowd, above the depression of the meadow, above the level of the rest of the Convocation, up the short slope, and then they spread in every direction.

That's magic, she thought with a growing sense of awe. *That's our magic, going out to touch every spot on the Earth. Spreading out to protect the air and water, to cleanse, to purify.*

A few moments later, the candle's flame changed, and the greenish dust was dissipating. The witches released hands, and the ones at the altar spoke the words that broke the circle. Season gave Kerry's hand an extra squeeze, and the beatific smile on her face, Kerry guessed, probably matched her own. She could barely believe that she had been part of something like that, something that gave back to the planet from which she had taken so much. They had celebrated nature, and spring, and themselves, all at once. But their celebration had not been an empty gesture, simple praise or lip service. It had included specific and concrete action designed to improve the world they lived in, or at least to help it withstand the ravages of their own kind.

As she walked back up the hill in the company of her fellows, the glow of witch-light was accompanied by the inner glow of deep, lasting satisfaction.

This, she thought happily, *completely rules!*

14

That first full day ended in one of the many tents set up for dinner. If anything, the mood at the evening meal was even rowdier than the earlier ones—the tables were full, and someone at any given table seemed to know people at one of the others. The laughter was loud and long, the stories told hilarious and often bawdy. After the dishes were cleared away, people stayed in the tent, although not necessarily in their seats. Old friendships were reestablished and new ones struck. Kerry was treated like one of the gang. In general, the atmosphere was of a holiday meal with close family members, except that it was the biggest family Kerry had ever dreamed of.

The second day was much like the first. This time she felt more at ease, more familiar with her surroundings—ever-changing as they were—and a few times, she and Season split up to do different things. There was a lecture on growing herbs that Kerry wanted to attend, for instance, but Season wasn't that interested and said she had a business meeting that overlapped it. The Convocation wasn't just a fair and a celebration, it was a time of examining the past and planning for the future. This was the only area Kerry felt shut out of, but she figured that she was so new at the whole witch game that she wouldn't have much to offer that would be useful.

The whole thing was eye-opening. She had never imagined that witches came in such a vast assortment of shapes, sizes, colors, nationalities, and temperaments. Given her experience with Season and Mother Blessing, she had assumed that there would be a lot more infighting and treachery than what she had encountered here so far. Her perception, born of hard experience, was that witches were constantly at war with each other, which didn't seem to be the case at all.

The infighting didn't happen until the third day.

When that morning broke, it felt just like the one before. The golden light of magic filled the air, and Kerry's spirits felt lighter than ever, as if her very soul had been tethered to the earth but had now been set free. She woke up soaring.

Season's demeanor that day was different, however.

From the minute she got up, it seemed there was a weight on her. Her smiles were forced and artificial. Even her posture was a little slumped. She wore a conservative white blouse with black pants and boots and tied her hair back in a tight ponytail, a look that was a little formal and severe for her.

Kerry knew what the problem was, of course. Today was the Witches' Tribunal. Her case against Mother Blessing—or Mother Blessing's against Season—would be heard. She wasn't clear on which was the defendant and which the plaintiff. Then again, if it hadn't been for courtroom shows on TV, she wouldn't have known the difference anyway, her own life having been mercifully trial-free. She guessed it didn't much matter. The important thing was that Season would have her say, and justice would be meted out.

After breakfast she accompanied Season to the Tribunal—a vast open-air pavilion with several hundred seats set up in a configuration not unlike a TV courtroom's. They sat about halfway back and observed while several other cases came up on the docket. The Tribunal itself consisted of five witches, dour-faced, gray-haired eminences one and all, as opposed to the jovial group outside this pavilion. Season explained in hushed tones that it was deliberate—to sit on the Tribunal, one had to be a witch of considerable experience and wisdom, having attended at least three previous Convocations. Away from the Tribunal grounds, these justices might be as carefree as any other witch, but while they worked they kept serious demeanors to indicate the care with which they did the job and the respect they held for accusers and accused alike.

In this crowd, however, no one wore black robes, and that included the jurists of the Tribunal. They wore long, flowing robes, but two were of a deep forest green, one of darkest midnight blue, and two a rich wine color. The robe colors might have had some significance, but if so, Kerry wasn't told what it was.

The cases mostly involved matters that seemed minor to Kerry—the equivalent of small claims court or disputes over whose dog was using whose yard as a restroom. One male witch was accused of having counteracted the spell of a female for no reason except that he was angry because her dog had beat up his at a picnic. He claimed that her dog had been a vicious brute who should have been put down, but even so, that was not the reason he had counteracted her spell—it was because he had been asked to by the person her spell was directed at. Doing so, he declared, was perfectly legal under the witches' code of justice.

The judges agreed with his argument, but they still faulted him for not having communicated with her directly before countering her spell. Both witches were directed to do volunteer work in their community—nothing witchy about it, simply labor in the service of the people among whom they lived. All in all, Kerry decided, it was a lot like watching an extended episode of *Judge Judy,* except that the justices were less annoying and there were no commercial breaks.

By the time Season's case came up, however,

she was having to stifle her yawns. Everything had been so orderly, so composed, that it was all a little dull. She knew that the dispute between Season and Mother Blessing was made of juicier stuff, and she guessed that many of the other spectators in the place were there to watch it unfold.

The justice at the far left of the bench, one of the two men, called Season Howe and Myrtle Blessing—one of the few times Kerry had ever heard her referred to as anything but Mother Blessing—to the front. Both women rose and advanced, though Mother Blessing's legs seemed to have gotten worse—she relied more heavily on the cane, and she had a noticeable limp, accompanied by several winces and even a groan or two. Kerry thought the whole thing way over-the-top theatrical, and couldn't believe she was laying it on so thick. Surely the justices would see through it.

But instead, the one in the center—the oldest, judging from normal, non-witchy standards, which Kerry understood to be meaningless in this instance—tossed her a look of profound and genuine sympathy. "I'm sorry to put you through this, Mother Blessing," she said. "And I trust we will resolve this matter swiftly and to everyone's satisfaction."

"That's all I'm hopin' for too," Mother Blessing said. Even the cornpone Southern accent had been intensified for the occasion. Mother Blessing was obviously going to play every card at her disposal, and then some.

"I'm sure that's the result all of us will work toward," Season said. She sounded intelligent and articulate. Kerry hoped that didn't work against her—the city slicker trying to take advantage of the down-home gal. Both parties to the action were directed to sit at the front of the gallery, between the bench and the spectators. Season took her seat primly, with her legs crossed and her hands folded in her lap, while Mother Blessing practically sprawled into hers.

The center jurist, the one wearing the dark blue robe, glanced at a piece of paper, as if reminding herself of the nature of the case, and then addressed Mother Blessing. *Or Myrtle,* Kerry thought with a private smile.

"Mother Blessing, we are here to consider an event that occurred in the year 1704, in the place known as Slocumb, Virginia. Were you present at that event?"

"Durn tootin'," Mother Blessing said, provoking a raucous laugh from the audience, if not from the justices.

"And would you tell us what you remember about that event, including specifically the role that Season Howe played in it?"

"Yes," Mother Blessing said, more sober now. "I will."

She spent the next half hour telling the Tribunal pretty much the same story Kerry had read in Daniel's journals, adding some of the details that Daniel had apparently not known but that she had mentioned to Kerry. There were even a couple that Kerry hadn't heard before. For instance, when she described how Season had gone berserk and started magically blasting townsfolk, including her husband, Winthrop Blessing, she mentioned that Season had specifically singled Winthrop out, shouting, "You'll never live to spread your lies about me!" at him as she reversed his own musket ball into his brain.

With the exception of those embellishments, however, it was the same story Kerry had heard before. When witchcraft was determined to be the cause of the deaths of the Flinders children, both of the town's witches were suspected. Mother Blessing cooperated with the investigation, while Season Howe flew into an unreasonable fury, answering even the most innocuous questions with violence and death. The more she raged, the more furious she became, feeding on her own anger in some sort of escalating feedback loop. Finally, Mother Blessing, to save her own life and the lives of her unborn sons, had taken refuge deep in the Swamp. Season had continued her rampage even after everyone in town was dead, burning each house and starting a fire that burned for months, feeding off the peat that grew in the Swamp.

By the time she had finished her tale, tears streamed down Mother Blessing's face, smearing her eyeliner into twin black rivers. "I didn't dare come out of the Swamp for a month, maybe more, your honors," she declared. "When I finally did, and went to look at the town where I had lived, where my husband had died, where my sons had been conceived, the ground was still hot to the touch. Nothin' grows on that soil to this day, and you'll never convince me that anything will. It's cursed land, blasted and scorched by the explosive temper of . . ."—here she lowered her gaze, as if she was afraid to look directly at Season, and ticked her head toward her foe instead—". . . of Season Howe."

Kerry glanced around the pavilion. Faces were serious, reflective. Mother Blessing had told her story well, tossing in whatever theatrics she could to make sure it played to the room. People seemed to believe her. Kerry noticed a few spectators eyeing Season carefully, as if she might throw a murderous fit right here before the Tribunal.

"Is there anything else you would like to add?" one of the justices asked Mother Blessing.

"Only that both of my sons, blessed be their spirits, were later murdered by Season Howe for the crime of tryin' to find her and bring her to some kind of justice."

"Justice is why the Tribunal exists," another jurist pointed out. "It is not yours to deliver."

Mother Blessing sniffled and dabbed at her eyes with a formerly white handkerchief that had turned ash gray. "It's not so easy to tell a pair of grievin' boys that, your honor. Ones who never got the chance to know their daddy in this life."

"I'm sure that's true," the jurist replied.

"Season Howe," the justice in the center intoned. "You stand accused. How plead you?"

Season had sat quietly through Mother Blessing's entire monologue. Kerry thought it must have been difficult to resist rolling her eyes at some of the more obvious whoppers, or laughing out loud from time to time, but Season had managed. She maintained an air of dignity even as she turned in her seat to face the bench.

"I plead not guilty, your honor, and request the Tribunal's permission to state my case."

The justice nodded. "By all means," she said.

Season cleared her throat and began. "My daughter speaks the truth, up to a point," she said. "We did both live in Slocumb at that time. She did reside with her husband, Winthrop Blessing. What she didn't mention—what she apparently never mentions when she tells this tale—was that they had a first son, whom she named Darius. I had followed the tradition of giving my daughter a name from nature, but as you can see, that is but one of the many ways in which she chose to differentiate herself from me. When my former husband, Forest, heard about Darius, he came to Slocumb to meet his first grandchild. Forest was an evil witch, as I'm sure many of you will remember. Cruel, heartless, cold, and dedicated to dark pursuits."

There was a murmur of recognition and assent from the crowd—apparently Forest Howe's unpleasant reputation had not been forgotten.

"In Slocumb," Season continued, "Forest's influence over Myrtle grew quickly. I had tried to keep them separated from the time I first learned of Forest's true nature—sadly, only after Myrtle was born—but they were both adults now and I couldn't prevent them from being together. Myrtle, it turned out, was her father's daughter, much more than mine.

"Mother Blessing's version of events that followed is true again, up to a point. The widow Flinders did awaken to find her children brutally murdered. The townspeople did rouse the two of us, the two prominent witches in town—but not to question us.

Instead, they wanted us both dead, right then and there, no questions asked. There had been earlier incidents, no doubt games Forest and Myrtle played, and the town had had enough.

"Both of us fought back," Season went on. "The townsfolk were prepared for resistance, and battle was joined. In the fight, the townspeople killed Forest and young Darius, and Myrtle simply became unhinged. From that point, everything she attributes to me was, in fact, her doing. She killed every living soul in town. She blasted the houses, ruined the land, started the fires. People from nearby towns saw the smoke and came to help, and Myrtle accused me, told them I was a witch—in itself, one of the most serious crimes with which this Tribunal has to contend. I ran, to save myself. Ran and hid. I had been injured in the battle, could barely escape with my life. But I left only after the town was razed by her magic. She claims to have run before the town was destroyed, yet she knows precisely the progression of events. How would she know? She never told a soul, including her other sons, Daniel and Abraham, about Darius and Forest. She didn't tell this Tribunal. But you all remember Forest. Do you recall any instance of him appearing after 1704? Do you know how he died, unless you've heard it from me? You certainly have never heard it from Myrtle, who has conveniently forgotten that she ever had a father."

She stopped then, regarded the audience impassively, and even let her gaze sweep across her daughter.

After a respectful period, the center justice spoke again. "Mother Blessing," she said. "You have now heard Season Howe's rebuttal to your testimony. Do you have anything you wish to add?"

"Durn—I mean, I sure do, your honor," Mother Blessing replied, garnering another laugh. Not as big as the first one, though. By now, the crowd was caught up in the drama of the moment. "No, I did not mention the fact that Season Howe is my mother—a fact I try hard to forget every day of my life. I didn't mention my father, either, because he wasn't there when all this happened. I don't have the first clue how he died—she made sure that I never really got to know him. Just like my boys never got to know Winthrop. Almost seems like she has somethin' against fathers and sons, doesn't it? As for this 'Darius,' I reckon she made him up out of whole cloth. Go ahead and examine the records—you won't find the birth of any Darius Blessing ever reported."

"We have inspected the records, in consideration of this account," one of the jurists who hadn't yet spoken announced. "And it is true, there has never been any report of the birth or death of Darius Blessing."

Mother Blessing gave a satisfied nod at that pronouncement, and a ripple of talk rushed through the pavilion.

"Season Howe?" the middle justice asked, raising her voice to be heard over the crowd.

"I'm sure the lack of responsibility Myrtle demonstrates by not having properly reported the birth and death of her first son will not be construed as evidence of anything but that simple fact," Season said.

"Very well," the center jurist said. "We will deliberate."

They left Season and Mother Blessing sitting in the front of the room while the justices put their heads together and spoke in low tones. They had done the same with the day's other cases, but Kerry thought this one probably deserved a more careful and spirited debate than those simple ones.

After only a few minutes, however, they broke their huddle and addressed the crowd. "We have been unable to arrive at a conclusion," the eldest announced. "Both stories have the ring of truth to them, although clearly both cannot be true. If there is more evidence to be presented, the Tribunal would be willing to hear it."

Mother Blessing spoke up first. "I really don't know what more y'all could possibly need," she said. "It's plain as day that she's lyin'. Just look at her."

The audience reacted with a surprised chuckle at her audacity. Horrifyingly, Kerry was afraid her pronouncement might have the desired effect. She saw some of the audience, as well as the Tribunal, examining Season as if looking for a big red L to appear on her forehead.

When the laughter faded, Season took her turn to address the Tribunal. "Myrtle's argument doesn't seem particularly compelling to me," she said. "I'd like to suggest a more definitive approach. I hereby request a Viewing."

Kerry didn't know what a Viewing was, but she could tell by the universal gasp of astonishment that it was not standard everyday Tribunal procedure.

"That's highly irregular, Season," the center justice declared. "Not without precedent, but unusual to say the least."

"I appreciate that," Season said.

"Not only is it unusual," the justice went on, "but I'm not certain we can accommodate the request. You are aware of the level of power and proficiency required for a Viewing?"

"I am," Season affirmed.

"You could not possibly accomplish it on your own," the justice said. "Mother Blessing could legitimately be a party to it, but the Tribunal can't force her to merge her power with yours, and given the circumstances—"

"Uh-uh. No way," Mother Blessing interrupted. "I ain't lettin' her get inside of me."

"As I suspected," the justice said. "The Tribunal itself cannot be a party to such an action, since we have to be free to see and interpret for ourselves. Unless you have some other suggestion—"

"I do," Season said, also interrupting. She turned her head, and her gaze caught Kerry's, bored into her. "I request that the Tribunal allow Kerry Profitt to participate."

15

Kerry felt her cheeks crimson as every eye in the pavilion fell on her. "Me?" she asked, fully aware that it was a cliché even as she said it. Surely there was no other Kerry Profitt around. And if there had been, just as surely Season would have mentioned the coincidence to her.

So the only out was if she had misheard altogether.

Since Season's gaze was fixed on her, and a slight smile curved her red lips, she didn't think that was the case. Kerry couldn't hear her voice over the buzz in the pavilion, but the word on her mouth was unmistakable. "You."

Kerry realized that her left hand was stupidly pointing at her own chest. "But—but I—" she stammered.

"Kerry Profitt," the center justice said, looking at Kerry as if she had only just crawled out from under something unsavory. The audience fell silent as she spoke. "She is . . . quite inexperienced, isn't she?"

"Maybe not as inexperienced as you might think," Season said.

"She does look very young," the male jurist on the end observed.

"She is young," Season admitted. "So were we all, once."

"A very good point."

Finally, Mother Blessing was able to do something with her mouth other than sit there with it hanging open. "I don't . . . I don't think that girl ought to be allowed to have anything to do with this," she declared.

"And why not, Mother Blessing?" one of the justices inquired.

"Because . . ." Kerry could see her trying to come up with some legitimate objection. "Because I taught her. I knew her before Season ever did."

"Well, then," the center justice noted, "you should be assured of her objectivity, isn't that right?"

Mother Blessing had opened her mouth and set her own trap. Kerry knew her well enough to recognize the look that crossed her face—the realization that she wasn't going to get her own way this time.

"All right," she said finally. "Let her try. We'll see if she has the stuff to pull it off."

The justices seemed satisfied by that. "Kerry Profitt," the eldest said, looking right at her. "Please approach the Tribunal."

As Kerry stood and made her way down her row of seats, various witches—some she had met over the past couple of days, others she had not—offered whispered encouragement. She was glad. Their confidence in her helped fight off the rubber knees, the dry throat, the quavering hands, as she stood before the bench.

"I'm Kerry Profitt."

"Do you know Season Howe?" the middle justice asked.

"I do."

"And do you know Mother Blessing?"

"Yes, I do."

"And do you have reason to believe one of them more than the other, in this case?"

"Definitely," Kerry said.

"Season Howe has asked for your assistance with a Viewing. It won't be easy. It will be a strain on you, physically, mentally, and emotionally. Your power will be linked with Season's. The two of you will be allied, for the duration of the Viewing, more closely than most people ever are with anyone—right down to the center of your being. This is necessary, however, because no witch lives who can manifest a Viewing by herself. Two very powerful witches can do it, three or more is better. Are you willing to participate in the way that I've described?"

Kerry swallowed. She still couldn't quite believe that Season had selected her for this. There must have been dozens of witches in this pavilion alone who were better suited for it.

But she asked for me.

"I am."

"And are you prepared to let this Tribunal see whatever there is to see, without trying to warp or alter the reality we are being shown?"

She hadn't even known she could alter any

reality at all. But then, she still wasn't really clear on what the Viewing entailed. "I am."

"Very well," the jurist said. "This Tribunal calls for a Viewing."

Another buzz from the audience. Apparently a Viewing was a big deal, not something they experienced every day, or maybe even every Convocation. Kerry had the sense of having been swept up in something huge.

Season held out her hand to Kerry, who took it. Season gave hers a squeeze. "You'll be fine," she said quietly. "Don't worry about a thing."

"Just let me know what to do," Kerry said. "I'll give it my best shot."

"Just follow my lead," Season said. "We won't be alone for long."

Kerry wondered what she meant by that but didn't get a chance to ask her. Season took Kerry's other hand and held both tightly. She closed her eyes. Kerry did the same, but not before catching a glimpse of Mother Blessing watching them with a scowl, arms crossed over her expansive bosom. She looked like she wished they were both dead, which she no doubt did, having tried numerous times to achieve exactly that result.

As soon as Kerry's eyes were closed, though, she felt something like a powerful electrical current running through her hands and up her arms. The charge traveled into her shoulders, across her back, then down her spine, through her body, down her legs. She was aware of the fine hairs on her arms and legs standing on end, aware of the air brushing against her skin, aware of every inch of fabric that covered her and the weight of her hair against her back. The smells of the pavilion—the odors of people, flowers, soaps, perfumes, sweat, dirt, even the wood of the chairs—filled her senses. She thought she could hear the breathing and the beating heart of everyone in the place.

But then all those things fell away, as if she had shot up into the air and left everything behind. The sounds were replaced by a rushing noise, the smells by a coppery, electrical scent, and the sensations against her skin vanished completely, as if she had stepped out of her own body.

She was tempted to open her eyes and see

what was going on. But Season had said to follow her lead, so she would not open her eyes until she was told to.

As it turned out, she didn't have to. Another moment of darkness passed. A dizzying feeling of vertigo struck her, a wave of nausea that was gone as quickly as it had come. Then her eyes were open of their own volition, and her vision filled with greens, every shade of green: the pale, almost yellow color of new leaves; the dark bluish tinge of fir trees by moonlight; the rich velvet of freshly cut grass, and everything in between. Gradually, shapes delineated themselves in the field of greens, and she realized she was looking at the Great Dismal Swamp, with its tall trees, its thick, almost impenetrable layers of underbrush, its stagnant pools, its hanging mosses.

More disconcerting still was the fact that *through* the Swamp she could see the Tribunal pavilion. It was as if she was looking into a window at night, with the light on the other side—one level of view showed the Swamp, but another one showed where her body stood, hands clasped with Season's. She could even turn her head and take in the bench,

Mother Blessing, the audience, without affecting her view of the Swamp. The whole thing made her dizzy again.

When the eldest justice spoke, her voice was muffled as if by distance, but Kerry could still make out the words. For the first time she realized that the people attending the Tribunal could see what she was seeing—at least they could see the Swamp part of it. This, then, was the Viewing—somehow, she and Season were projecting an image of the Swamp for them.

"You are showing us Slocumb, Virginia, on October twentieth of the year 1704?"

"We are." Season's voice, sounding closer than the justice's.

The image seemed still, static, and Kerry wondered how it could possibly be of any use to the Tribunal. But almost as soon as she thought it, as if in response, there was motion—a figure breaking through the trees, approaching them. A man. He was dressed in modern clothing, not the garb of the eighteenth century. A clean white shirt, sleeves rolled up over tanned forearms. Faded jeans. Brown hair swept away from his forehead. Gray eyes that twinkled as if he had just thought of a private joke. A smile that carved crags in his cheeks.

Daniel!

"Hello, Kerry," he said as he neared them. "It's so good to see you, even . . . even this way."

"I—I don't quite know what to say," Kerry confessed, her heart fluttering against her ribs like a bird in a delicate cage. "You're . . ."

He chuckled. "A sight for sore eyes? Dead? Both?"

In the pavilion, Season released Kerry's hands.

In the Swamp, Daniel took them, lifted one to his lips, pressed it there. Then he let it go and encircled Kerry with his arms. She moved into the hug, and she felt—really felt!—his body, the familiar solidity of his muscular form, the warmth. She could see Season standing beside her, watching with a happy smile.

"This is . . . kind of overwhelming, Daniel," she said. "I mean, I'm thrilled to see you, but . . ."

"I understand," Daniel said sympathetically. "It's not what you were expecting. The Viewing requires a Guide, and Season asked me if I would fill that role. Knowing I would get to see you, I happily agreed. And since my passing, I've come to learn the truth about Slocumb, so I'm happy to share that truth here."

Kerry risked a glance around the pavilion. Daniel wasn't there, so he existed only in the reality represented by the Swamp. "I guess I just don't get how all this stuff works," she admitted.

"No one expects you to yet. You will, in time. Just remember, death is a passage, not a destination."

"So you've told me," she said with a cheerful giggle. The realization that she was genuinely talking to Daniel filled her with a joy she could barely contain.

It took Season to remind her of the serious nature of their activity. "We should get to work," she said firmly.

"Right," Daniel agreed. He gestured behind Kerry, and she turned around.

As she did, the view shifted, and she knew the whole Tribunal audience was seeing what she did. Behind her stood the village of Slocumb as it had on that cold October day. A bitter wind rustled the trees and a rare dusting of snow powdered the ground and the rooftops. The houses were mostly wood-framed, although a few were built of stone or brick. Every one had a prominent chimney, and smoke leaked from most of those. Roofs were steeply pitched and interrupted by gables. Most of the houses were shallow, Kerry guessed only a single room deep.

Daniel led the way toward the village, Kerry and Season following right behind. None of them spoke now, and though Kerry thought she should be able to hear the sound of their feet crunching the frozen earth, their progress was silent. All she heard was the rush of the wind in the trees.

And then the quiet was split by a shattering scream from an open window of the nearest house.

The scene shifted, and they were inside that house. A woman—Kerry knew her at once as the widow Flinders—stared into her children's room, her hands clutching her cheeks in horror. Inside the room was a scene that Kerry didn't want to see. She knew what was there, had already caught a glimpse of blood, shockingly red on the hardwood floor. Kerry tried to keep her gaze riveted on the widow. As awful as the woman's horrified pose was, it wasn't as bad as what was inside the room. Her three children brutally savaged, torn apart with animal fury. The widow Flinders screamed again and ran through the room to the open window, as if whoever was responsible might still be standing outside.

The widow screamed again, louder. In the snow outside were the tracks of a large canine. A wolf, Kerry thought. But the children's room was on the second floor of the house, the window a gabled one set into the roof. How could a wolf have climbed up to that room to do this work?

The widow's screams roused the town. Soon people came running from every direction. Mostly men, many carrying weapons or tools that could be pressed into such service— axes, hoes, muskets. They called to her, and when she couldn't answer, having succumbed to great, wracking sobs and fallen into a heap on her floor, some of them rushed into her house.

Before Kerry had to look at the carnage again, the scene shifted once more. She had the sense that this was Daniel's doing, that his role as Guide was to lead them around, highlighting the most significant events for the benefit of the Tribunal. Now they were outside a house that Kerry knew was Mother Blessing's. Some of the townsfolk, led by a man who had to be Parson Coopersmith, rapped on the door of that house. They looked apprehensive, their weapons bristling toward the door as if they could hide behind them.

Mother Blessing opened the door, looking much as Kerry knew her. The wind fluttered her white cotton nightdress around her. She was a little younger, a little smaller than she was now, but still she dwarfed the man—Winthrop Blessing, no doubt—who tried to crowd into the doorway beside her. There was a brief, clearly antagonistic exchange between the Blessings and the parson, following which she closed the door. Barely a second later—Kerry understood that Daniel was compressing events to a certain degree—she reappeared at the door, this time dressed in a dark, high-collared dress and heavy black shoes. As soon as she stepped out, Parson Coopersmith grabbed one of her arms, and a burly man took hold of the other. Weapons were pointed at her. Winthrop looked on in horror as his wife was led away. Another man shoved Winthrop aside—a man with a ragged, wild look, an unkempt beard, and an infant in his arms. That was Forest Howe, Kerry knew. With young Darius. Forest stalked behind the group taking Mother Blessing away, shouting at them. Kerry was glad she couldn't hear the words.

Another whirlwind shift, and a similar scene played out at Season Howe's house. Season came out fully dressed, with a cap over her blond hair and a brown dress belted around her slender waist. As with Mother Blessing, she was taken captive immediately upon her emergence.

Shift again. Slocumb's town square. Witches being hauled in from two directions. Mother Blessing scowling, tugging, trying to free herself, while Season cooperated, chatting almost casually with those who led her.

Mother Blessing tore an arm free from her captors and pointed accusingly at Season. Parson Coopersmith flinched from her, and apparently that simple action ignited her fury. Now Daniel let them hear her words, screamed in rage. "So you believe that I am a witch,

Parson? I'll show you what a witch can do! You should be glad I have suffered you for so long!"

Parson Coopersmith was almost blubbering as he replied. "M—Mother Blessing, there is no need f—for—"

But she cut him off with a simple gesture and a magical blast that Kerry had seen before. "*Hastamel!*" Mother Blessing shouted. A burst of energy expelled from her hands and struck Parson Coopersmith in the center of the chest, rolling through him like a cannonball.

The square was still for a moment, as bits of the parson pattered down on the cobblestones like a heavy rain. Then the townspeople turned on both Season and Mother Blessing, as if they had been equally responsible for the clergyman's demise. A pitchfork's tines drove into Season's ribs before she could even react. Musket balls flew. Axes were swung. Season defended herself magically, even as blood gushed from her initial wound. She drew back to a more defensible position, with the chimney of a nearby house at her back.

Mother Blessing, meanwhile, stood her ground in the center of the square, hurling spells in every direction. Bits of the parson still clung to her cheeks and dress. The townsfolk reacted in kind—trying to shoot her from a distance, prying cobblestones up from the square and throwing them at her. Forest and Darius were spotted at the edge of things, Forest tossing out spells of his own, and the attack was expanded to include him. A musket ball slammed into his shoulder, a cobblestone tore a gash in his forehead, and then he and the child both went down under a mob of townspeople wielding flashing blades and heavy objects. Mother Blessing saw this happen, and her fury visibly grew, her cheeks purpling, her mouth working in incoherent rage.

Season abandoned her position by the chimney and tried to approach Mother Blessing. Her posture and expression were consoling, as if she were trying to calm the other witch. But Mother Blessing wanted none of it, and she drove Season back with wave after wave of magical attacks that Season, injured and weakened, could barely withstand.

Kerry could see the intensity of Mother Blessing's frenzy spiraling out of control. She no longer cared where she aimed her attacks—Kerry wasn't sure she could even see anymore, or if she had been blinded by her own furor. Magical energy swirled around her in a kind of tornado that echoed what must have been going through her twisted mind. The power of her assault tore bricks from houses, ripped boards from their walls and sent them sailing into the Swamp, yanked shingles from their roofs. The dead in the square outnumbered the living now, and not even the people hiding in their own homes were safe from the onslaught.

Kerry looked away from the incredible scene and toward the Tribunal, where she saw faces in shock, aghast at what they were observing. It was obvious to everyone now, Kerry was sure, whose version of the day's events was more accurate.

And while she watched, unable to move or speak on that plane of reality, unable to do anything to intercede, she saw Mother Blessing leave her seat. Arms reached out to stop her but she deftly evaded them. She held something in her right hand—it took Kerry a moment to recognize it as a knife—and she raised it high as she lunged at Season.

Kerry felt the cold steel slicing into

Season's breast as surely as if it had been her Mother Blessing had stabbed, felt the shock and pain as the knife's keen blade drove into Season's heart.

Connected to Season, she knew every bit of Season's agony as the life ebbed out of her.

16

In Slocumb the Season who stood with Kerry and Daniel opened her mouth in a surprised-looking O shape. A red spot blossomed on her white blouse, spreading like a rose opening its petals, and then a single drop trailed down the outside of the blouse.

In the Tribunal pavilion, Season made a small whimpering sound. Her eyes rolled back in her head and she collapsed to the floor as if all her muscles had failed her at once.

Kerry couldn't catch her breath. "She stabbed you," she said, but it came out as little more than a squeak.

"I know," Slocumb's Season said, more calmly but still with an edge of worry. She raised a hand to her blouse, touched her chest. The hand came away bloody.

"Season," Daniel said urgently, reaching for her.

"It's okay, Daniel," she assured him.

Kerry had been astonished by many things over the past few days—*make that several months,* she mentally amended—but few things surprised her like the sight of Daniel embracing Season and then drawing away with her blood staining his own crisp shirt. "I am sorry," he said. "For so much."

"You did what you believed was right," she assured him. "No one could expect more than that."

He glanced toward his mother, who in Slocumb was directing her power against what was left of the small town. Houses had been torn apart as if by hurricane winds. Most of the buildings were ablaze now. Nothing living still moved, as far as Kerry could see. "I was . . . I was wrong. We all were."

Season winced—she was still upright in this reality, but the pain she felt was evident. "Now you know. Now everybody does."

Kerry's own discomfort had lessened, becoming a deep, persistent ache instead of the sharp pain it had been at first. She guessed that she had felt it because she and Season were linked, but then as Season faded in the real world—at least, what she perceived as the real world—that connection was broken and the agony became less distinct.

But was Season dead, in that world? And if so, what did that mean for Kerry? Would she be able to get back there?

In that world Kerry could see that the other witches in the audience at the Tribunal had restrained Mother Blessing, wrenching the knife from her grasp and hauling her away from Season's fallen body. On that plane Kerry could only stand there watching Season bleed on the ground. Some witches had gathered around her body and were performing healing spells, and one of them helped move Kerry out of the way.

"Are you . . . are you dying, Season? That knife couldn't really hurt you, could it?" Kerry remembered Mother Blessing firing four bullets into Season's chest, and Season spitting them out into her hand.

"It's within the grounds of the Convocation," Season explained. "It's as infused with magic as everything else there. I'm afraid it was a very effective attack."

"But . . . how effective?" Kerry demanded. "You can't . . ."

Even as she spoke she could see the witches in the pavilion pulling back away from Season's lifeless form. One of them brought out a length of white linen from somewhere and laid it reverently over Season's body.

Once again Kerry's moorings had been yanked away from her. The deaths of her parents, then Daniel, now Season—it seemed that every time she became attached to someone, that someone was taken away. She didn't want to make Season's death be all about her, but it was a disturbing reality just the same.

Then she felt Daniel's comforting hand on her shoulders. "A passage, Kerry," he reminded her. "Not a destination."

"I'm standing here talking to you, right?" Season said.

"Yes, but . . . I'm confused," Kerry complained. Behind them Mother Blessing's Slocumb rampage continued, but no one was watching it—the witch was just as alone now as she had been on that fateful day.

"And you have every right to be." Season rubbed her arm, and with her and Daniel consoling Kerry, she realized she felt almost okay about it. "Life is a wonderful thing, Kerry," Season went on. "And you should embrace it every day. You should look at each new dawn as another opportunity, another promise of hope and love and miracles, and you should look at the stars at night the same way. But life—the kind of life you're thinking about—doesn't last forever. For anyone. Not even witches."

"She's right," Daniel added. "Which is why you need to make the most of every minute you do have."

"Do you understand how incredibly powerful you are, Kerry?" Season asked her. "Not one witch in a hundred could have worked with me to pull off a Viewing. But I had every faith in you, and you pulled it off. You've accomplished every task I've ever put before you. Now I'm asking you to do one more thing."

"What?"

"Go back into your world. Be the best witch you can be, and the best person you can be. Put your abilities to work in the service of something good, something lasting and true. I don't know what that should be, but you'll find it if you look."

"That's all?"

Season and Daniel both laughed. "A lot of people don't seem to be able to do that much," Daniel said. "If you can, you're ahead of the game. But I know you will."

"But . . . but I'll miss you guys so much," Kerry said. "Both of you are the most—"

"We'll be there when you need us, Kerry," Season interrupted.

"And you've been to this plane now," Daniel put in. "You can come back, you know. Drop in from time to time. We'd love to see you, and I know Rebecca, Josh, and Mace would as well. Your parents, too."

The awful reality of Rebecca's death struck Kerry with sickening certainty. Her head spun with the ideas and possibilities they were laying before her. "I guess I still have a whole lot to learn about this stuff."

"You do indeed," Season agreed. "And you can't do that here. You need to go back now."

Kerry glanced into the Tribunal pavilion. Season's body was being taken out, elevated over the shoulders of those carrying her. She could see tears there, but also smiles and laughter. She thought they were remembering Season as she had been, sparkling, full of life and good cheer.

"Go," Daniel urged. "Everything will be fine."

Kerry looked at them both, not wanting to leave them behind, but knowing she had to.

She closed her eyes and centered herself. Willed herself to feel the power that surged inside her.

A sharp drop, a moment's vertigo . . .

And then she was back in the pavilion, with its million aromas, its crush of people, its voices.

Its life.

"Welcome back, Kerry Profitt." That was the center jurist, the eldest one, smiling at her from the bench. "You performed admirably."

"But . . . Season . . ."

"Has moved on," the jurist confirmed, nodding.

Kerry looked around for Mother Blessing. As if guessing who she sought, the male justice on the end said, "She has been taken into custody. Thanks to you, Season, and Daniel, this Tribunal now knows the truth about what happened in Slocumb, and that the blame for all those deaths, all that destruction, rests with Myrtle Blessing. Further, we know of the crimes Myrtle Blessing has committed to cover that one up—the sacrifices of her sons and the many more deaths, over the intervening years, for which she is responsible. And, of course, her murder of Season Howe, right here in our own presence. She will be held accountable for all these crimes."

"What's going to happen to her?" Kerry wanted to know.

The justices looked at each other, as if not sure they wanted to tell her. Finally, the eldest spoke up. "She has committed crimes of the most grievous nature. She has shown no remorse, given no indication that she is willing to stop her criminal actions. She will be stripped of her power." The jurist paused for a second, then added, "All of it."

Kerry considered that for a moment, tried to imagine what it would mean. Mother Blessing unable to manipulate others, manipulate the very Earth to do her bidding? She would be—

Wait a minute, Kerry thought, the true

meaning of the justice's words becoming clear to her. "But she's hundreds of years old!"

The senior jurist nodded. Kerry thought maybe there was the briefest glimmer of a smile on her face. Just for a split second. "No one said she would enjoy the process."

Kerry stood before the bench, speechless for a moment, horrified at the possibility. Before she could fully compose her thoughts, the justice banged three times on the bench with the palm of her hand. "I declare this Witches' Tribunal adjourned until tomorrow!" she shouted. "And I further declare that it's time for dinner!"

This declaration was greeted by a loud whoop of approval from the crowd. Kerry started for the nearest exit but was caught by a few of the audience members, who offered congratulations and support. Each one held her hands or hugged her, and then more came over, and still more, and then there was a mob around her, and more hugs, and more, and more, and more.

And that was just the beginning of the fun.

17

Kerry had gone inside the little caravan to change clothes for dinner and the evening's celebration, and to grab a few quiet moments to herself after the drama of the Tribunal and its raucous aftermath. At one point she caught a glimpse of Season's bed and then looked around expectantly, remembering even as she did that the trailer would be empty. She didn't quite know how to react for a minute. She had been with Season every day since Christmas Eve, and even before that she couldn't recall a day in which Season hadn't been on her mind from waking until sleep finally captured her again. Suddenly all that was over, and Season wouldn't be greeting her as faithfully as the sun and stars did any more.

Not only that, but the sun would never set

again on Daniel Blessing, or Rebecca Levine, or Mace Winston, or Josh Quinn. She had lost so much—they all had, really. Kerry was becoming convinced that what Daniel and Season had insisted was true: Death was just a passage to another level of existence, and not necessarily something to be mourned. But that didn't keep her from mourning her friends just the same. She figured that ultimately none of them would regret the price they had paid, since the end result was keeping Mother Blessing from continuing her destructive rampage across the land. Certainly plenty of innocents had already fallen victim to her misguided quest, but now at least no more would have to worry about that.

So Kerry tried to smile and greet the evening with the cheerful outlook Season would have wanted her to have. She put on a fresh, pale green frock, slipped sandals on her feet—both things one of the "shopkeepers" had insisted on giving her after the Tribunal was over—and went outside to dinner.

The first morning she had entered the meal tent feeling like a stranger, grateful that she had Season to cling to.

This time, though, she was hailed by at least a dozen people as soon as she had filled her tray. Hands full, she smiled and nodded to several and then sat down next to Tamsinn, a young woman from Pensacola she had met the evening before. Tamsinn was blithesome, with close-cropped purple hair and a ready smile. She greeted Kerry with a grin and a squeeze.

"Are you okay?" she asked. "I know this afternoon was rough on you."

"I think so," Kerry answered, as honestly as she could. "I mean, I'm sure I have a way to go before I'm really back to normal, whatever that is. But I'm not as wrecked as I would have thought either."

"That's good," Tamsinn said. She took a sip of her herbal tea and squinted at Kerry through the steam. "I know this whole deal can seem all huge and complicated when it's new."

"Yeah," Kerry agreed. "I'm definitely still at that stage."

"It'll go by fast," Tamsinn assured her. "Seems like I was there just the other day."

"How long has it been for you?"

Tamsinn scrunched her face up while she

did the math in her head. "I guess sixty-two years," she said finally.

Kerry was stunned, although she knew she shouldn't have been. She would have sworn Tamsinn was no more than a year or two older than her, if that. She had learned plenty of times that among the community of witches one couldn't guess age based on appearance. But she wondered, not for the first time, when she would reach the peak of her power, and where she would "freeze," in terms of appearance, as witches did.

"If there's anything you need, Kerry, any questions you have or anything like that, you just let me know, okay? I'll be happy to help. Me and about a thousand other witches, or more. We're here to help guide you, to teach you what we can, and to help you figure out what you're about."

"Thanks, Tamsinn," Kerry said. "That means a lot to me."

Both women resumed eating then, unable to resist the allure of the excellent meal. After dinner there would be a celebration, and then tomorrow, one more day of Convocation. There would be another day of Tribunal tomorrow as well, but she couldn't bring herself to go through that again. She had a feeling that she would cut out early tomorrow, go looking for Brandy and Scott. She needed to tell them about Rebecca, in case they didn't already know. And she found that she missed them a lot.

But before that, she had to finish her dinner.

And then there would be a party to remember.

Kerry lifted a forkful of fresh vegetables and tried to look at every spot in the tent, every face, every outfit, burning it all into her mind.

After all, five hundred years was a long time to wait until the next time.

She found Brandy and Scott at the While-a-Way Motel in Klamath Falls, Oregon, in a room on the second floor. A Harley Davidson convention seemed to have taken over the first, or at least the parking lot and swimming pool area: That didn't matter to Kerry—it wasn't hot enough for swimming yet anyway. The parking lot thing was a little more problematic, but she found street parking for the Raider and hiked in.

Scott threw the door open at her knock and dragged her inside, wrapped in his arms. Brandy joined him, and the three of them held each other for minutes before anyone was willing to break the hug. Kerry had always loved hugging, but her ribs were still a little sore after the lovefest that the last day and night of the Convocation had turned out to be. She had skipped the second day of the Tribunal in favor of trying to get acquainted with as many of her fellow witches as possible.

Finally, she was able to sit down on one of the beds. Brandy claimed the other, and Scott rolled over a wheeled chair from the little dining table. The room was motel basic, adequate for their needs but not much more than that. Kerry noted with a private grin that only one bed seemed to have been slept in. "So?" Scott began while she looked around. "We want to hear everything."

"So do I," Kerry replied. "But first, I should tell you about Rebecca. She's gone—Mother Blessing got her, as we feared. I don't suppose you found her body?"

Their faces fell instantly, so dramatically

that they really didn't need to say any more. Brandy did anyway. "We looked all over Santa Cruz for two days, called every hospital up and down the coast, called the morgues, bugged the cops until I thought they'd arrest us. She never turned up. At this point, I have to say I don't think she's going to."

"I'm sorry, Kerry," Scott added. "I know what she meant to you. To all of us, really."

Even though she had already known, talking about their friend felt like a shaft in the heart for Kerry, but she remembered what Daniel and Season had told her. *Just a passage.* She would have to explain that to Brandy and Scott if she could, and she hoped they would understand it without the visual aid that she'd had.

"I'm sorry too," Kerry said, leaving it there for the moment. "Season's dead, too. Mother Blessing killed her at the Convocation. It was awful. But Mother Blessing is being . . . held accountable, finally. For everything she's done. Slocumb, Daniel and Abraham, us. Everything."

"So . . . it's all over?" Scott asked, his voice tinged with excitement. Kerry couldn't tell if he was pleased, or maybe a little disappointed, that their long adventure was coming to a close.

"That part of it's over," she confirmed. "There's no more struggle between Season and Mother Blessing. No more looking over our shoulders, wondering who's coming for us next. We can finally relax, I guess."

"There's another part?" Brandy pressed. "What's left?"

"The part where I really am a witch now," Kerry said. "And remaining one, and working to develop my abilities."

She watched their faces carefully when she told them. Brandy's looked tentative, as if she was withholding judgment on Kerry's future plans. But Scott grinned like some kind of madman. "That's great!" he enthused. "I think you'll be such a good witch. Does that sound stupid? Kerry the good witch?"

"A little," Kerry said. "But I get what you mean, and thanks."

"I guess we should tell her our plans, too," Brandy said, leaning over to tap Scott's shoulder.

"I guess so," he agreed.

"'Our'? You guys have 'our' plans?"

"Well, we still have plenty of school to get through," Scott said. "Maybe even grad school, who knows? But the tentative plan is, as soon as we graduate, we get married. And then, as soon as we can, we start working on a family."

"I guess we're kind of used to having a lot of people around," Brandy said. "And a lot of excitement."

"And of course, Aunt Kerry is definitely a part of whatever family plans we make," Scott added.

Kerry laughed. "I'm an aunt already? The graduating part hasn't even happened yet."

"Well, when it does," Brandy clarified with a laugh. Kerry was thrilled to see the two of them looking so happy. Every time they glanced at each other, their gazes held. *They are definitely in love,* she thought.

Nothing wrong with that.

Kerry Profitt's diary, March 24.

They kept telling me that death is a passage, and okay, I can buy that.

What they didn't say is that there are plenty of other passages too. Scott and Brandy, starting a family? Scott and Brandy sitting in one room speaking civilly to each other would have been a lot to ask four months ago. I don't know if they'll really do it—who ever knows what's going to happen next week or next month, let alone two years from now? There are a lot of passages ahead for them, and maybe they'll weather them together. Maybe not. They'll be okay either way.

Maybe that's what Daniel and Season have left me with. I'm going to be fine. Scott and Brandy too. Things work out if you let them, if you work at them, if you help them along. And if you open your eyes and your mind and your heart to whatever each day brings. Sounds like something out of one of Brandy's pop psychology books, but there it is.

Anyway, I hope they do start a family, because it's been a while since I've really had one I could call my own. Now I'll have two—theirs, and the family of witches. The members of the Convocation took me in, embraced me, really made me feel that I was welcome there, wanted there even without being under Season's wing.

Of course, it's a long time until the next Convocation. There's a movement under way to hold them more often, maybe every hundred years instead of every five hundred. Easier to keep track of old friends, and new ones, that way. I'm voting in favor of it.

After the Tribunal, and the celebration that followed, I made my way back to our trailer, a little sad that Season wasn't in it with me but also happy, happier than I can remember being, oh, pretty much ever. Because there was a new sensation I was carrying around with me, and it wasn't the love of any particular individual, I realized, and it wasn't even my new understanding of my own power.

It was peace.

That's all. That simple.

I don't know what Scott and Brandy's future holds, and I don't know what mine does. I'm the new witch on the block, the new pawn in a very, very old game. Chaos and entropy on one side, order on the other.

But that's the future. That's tomorrow, and all the tomorrows after that.

For now, for tonight, I cling to peace.

And that's all I really need.

More later.

K.

The End

JEFF MARIOTTE is the author of more than twenty novels, including several set in the universes of *Buffy the Vampire Slayer*, *Angel*, *Charmed*, *Star Trek*, and *Andromeda*, the original horror novel *The Slab*, and more comic books than he has time to count, some of which have been nominated for Stoker and International Horror Guild awards. With his wife Maryelizabeth Hart and partner Terry Gilman he co-owns Mysterious Galaxy, a bookstore specializing in science fiction, fantasy, mystery, and horror. He lives on the Flying M Ranch in southeastern Arizona with his family and pets, in a home filled with books, music, toys, and other examples of American pop culture. More information than you would ever want to know about him is at www.jeffmariotte.com.

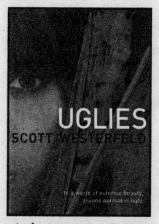

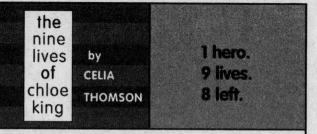

the nine lives of chloe king

by CELIA THOMSON

**1 hero.
9 lives.
8 left.**

It happened fast. Just a moment earlier, Chloe had been sitting with Amy and Paul on the observation deck atop Coit Tower in San Francisco. *What would happen if I dropped a penny from up here?* she wondered. She climbed up on the railing and dug into her jeans pocket, hunting for spare change.

That was when she fell.

As Chloe tumbled through the fog, all she could think was, *My mother will be so upset when she finds out I skipped school. . . . Maybe all that stuff about your life flashing before your eyes is just bull.*

Or maybe Chloe already knew, down in the unconscious depths of her mind, that she still had eight lives to go.

Don't miss this hot new series from Simon Pulse:

The Fallen

The Stolen

The Chosen

Published by Simon & Schuster

feel the fear.

A brand-new Fear Street trilogy by the master of horror

Coming in Summer 2005

Simon Pulse
Published by Simon & Schuster
FEAR STREET is a registered trademark of Parachute Press, Inc.